FAST

LANE

FRIENDS

Ron Neumer

Published in the United States of America
Two Suns Press

Cover design by Ron Neumer

ISBN: 978-0-9850928-7-0
Library of Congress No. 2015933030

DEDICATION

Ginny

Lisa

Jennifer

Kellen

Ashley

Kyle

Jessica

Sean

Alex

Don Brennan

Janet Cunningham, Ph.D.

and the late, Del Shannon

Patty

Thanks for your great friendship.

Ron

ACKNOWLEDGMENTS

Special thanks and gratitude to Don Brennan my former editor at Newsgleaner Publications. I am so grateful for his encouragement and guidance and for granting me the special title, "Staff Writer." Without this foundation, this book would never had been possible.

Thanks also to Dr. Janet Cunningham, my current editor and publisher. Janet believes in "synchronicity," and a chance encounter we had went a long way to seeing this book reach its completion.

Thank you both so much for helping me be a part of this great profession.

Thanks also to my wife, Ginny. While she was meditating, she came up with the title for the book. I was going nowhere on this. Thank you, sweetheart.

TABLE OF CONTENTS

Rico James Paradise
And
Arlene Marie Denali

To Find Real Love Or Tragedy

Damn grimy south bound freight train couldn't go any slower behind the century old five-story high power tool factory nationally renowned for the quality and durability of the "Made in America" product manufactured there. Connected together in the dusty railroad yards at the Frankford Junction Depot with empty box cars having their graffiti marred doors flung open, orange trimmed with black chemical cars showing signs of recent spillage, and low slung gondola cars heaped high aloft with twisted and rusted scrap metal, the sixty-car freight train gave off this annoying screeching sound going through trash littered switching tracks; and it seemed like the screeching would never stop and you just wanted to scream at whoever was driving the damn thing.

Then there was this relentless directly overhead going nowhere orange sun making everything hot to the touch, and it wasn't even the afternoon yet and weather forecasts indicated it was only going to get hotter and hotter as the day went on and you just might snap from the sweltering heat.

And somehow you could figure things out on your own without some smart-mouthed educated jerk pointing it out to you that this isn't a trendy Main Line area like those featured in some glossy sophisticated magazine targeted towards the cultured, affluent, and the soiree having in-crowd. Around here you won't find any street signs with lavish and moneyed-sounding names like *The Court at Avondale East* or *The Mews at Elan Down* with haughty high-society people living there and they have this propensity to look down on those who they deem as being "outside the realm of the financially well to do."

Maybe it just comes down to this basic fact: A trendy Main Line area doesn't have a century-old five-story high power tool factory (encased in worn-out bricks situated alongside a trash littered railroad right of way) giving off this incessant, over and over, iron-on-iron pounding noise. And if this isn't enough, this might add to the aura of the place; the factory gives off airborne factory dust and grit swirling out through exhaust fans in high up opened windows.

Some messed up neighborhood we have here.

Go ahead, feel that dust and grit on your clammy skin.

Just listen to the noise until it gives you a damn migraine.

Maybe you heard the police sirens late last night wailing on their way to quell a family ruckus at the Shumaker house on Bermuda Street.

Meet neighborhood smart-ass, tough guy, and the direct opposite of a cultured main liner, Rico James Paradise. Rico grew up having it in his mind that he had a striking resemblance to movie icon James Dean. But most folks in the neighborhood thought he was nothing more than a fresh kid strutting around sun-glassed, his brown hair tousled and unkempt, wearing tight fitting dungarees and black motorcycle boots while stashing his cigarettes in the rolled-up sleeve of his white tee-shirt. Now with a name like Rico James Paradise, you might think he was a hot stud movie actor, a hip-talking Dee-Jay on a hot hits radio station, or maybe even an astronaut out there in deep space.

Truth is, the smart-ass tough guy non-astronaut got up some five hours late for some mandatory Saturday overtime at the chemical plant located under the elevated train structure in the blue collar Kensington section of the city. Rico's been warned over and over again by his burly cigar-smoking supervisor on the loading dock at the chemical plant. "Shape the hell up and do what's right. Miss work again and you'll be signing for unemployment checks."

Rico's supervisor always had a hard one for him. Besides work related issues, he couldn't stand Rico's smart mouthed attitude.

Finally, the screeching freight train, the blasted late morning heat and the relentless factory noise woke Rico about a half-hour before noon, when he should have got up at six. What can you damn expect though when you get in after 3 a.m. liquored-up after a night out at the race track drinking bottled beer at the Turf Lounge and betting on the ponies, downing hard liquor and playing cards with the unsavory crowd, almost getting into a brawl with Raysel the *Neighborhood Bookie*, and there was something else and it had to do with a pretty girl with high cheekbones and intelligent eyes, but we'll let that go for the moment.

Rico woke up hung over and damp with perspiration having already transferred significant amounts of it to the musty sheet he slept on. He had this dry, lousy, cigarette and stale liquored taste in his mouth and he felt as if he was somehow secured to the bed by some kind of a tie down system. First thought that hit him with a start after the outside noise and the broiling heat turning his place into a second floor oven was, *So what! So they fire me! There's always another job out there somehow or somewhere.*

The "something else" will hit him in a minute. And on and off, it would trouble him for a long, long, time. There were times when he thought he was free and clear of it, but like personal demons it would keep coming back now and then and grab hold of him and torment him.

It was this: *What happened with Arlene last night?*

What happened with Arlene...?

Deep down inside, Rico knows what happened. He will never admit it. He just came up less than a man when things were being said about having a chance for something in his life.

Arlene Marie Denali, 29, had one main aspiration for her life. She just wanted someone who loved her to come home to her and take her in his arms and hold her close and keep her safe and secure. Even though she doesn't recall exactly how she heard it, or where she may have read it, Arlene believed this: *With love in your life, you can do great things.*

It's really not too much for anyone to ask for, just a basic human need. And if you should go through life without it, either the waiting at home for someone or the going home to someone you love, what do you have in your life that really counts? Somehow though, even at just 29, Arlene felt her dream was slipping away and getting more and more out of reach.

Rico rolled over coughing from deep in his chest a pack-and-a-half-a-day cigarette cough, and with some forced effort breaking free of whatever he imagined was tying him down, he sat up hunched over on the side of his bed still coughing and cursing the blasted heat while trying to figure out where he tossed his cigarettes when he got in at 3 a.m.

Not a refreshing breeze anywhere in Rico's sweat box apartment on James Street, straight across the street from the power tool factory and a short block away from the trash-littered railroad tracks. Side-by-side windows, flaunting yellowed and tattered at the edges pull-down shades, were nothing more than conduits for the heat and factory dust. Peeling off his damp and soiled tee-shirt almost glued to his clammy skin, Rico then used it to wipe sweat and grit from his face, arms, and the back of his neck.

Nice apartment Rico has for a hundred bucks a month. The furniture, manufactured by the *Hi-Grade Furniture Company*, was worn out and ready for pickup and delivery to the neighborhood thrift store. And it would be questionable if that agency would even accept it. Drab, faded slime green, best describes the color of the walls, and they made you feel as if you were in close proximity to a southern swamp. And in the center of all of this hundred dollar a month luxury, on Rico's dressing bureau, a glass ash tray the size of a hubcap for a diesel truck filled with crushed cigarette butts.

No prospect for the lush life here. None whatsoever.

There was one big advantage to Rico's second floor apartment on James Street, and there was no extra charge at all for it. Right down at the corner, no more than fifty steps away from his front door, recently remodeled and under new management, *Johnny Cee's Friendly Neighborhood Bar and Grille.* With this flashing neon sign in the window: "ICE COLD BEER ON TAP AND PACKAGED TO GO." And in the other window: "LIVE ENTERTAINMENT ON WEEKENDS."

How fucking convenient is that?

Cold beer on tap to stay and drink at the bar with the low I.Q. crowd, or brown bagged to go for a home alone binge; and live entertainment before a packed house on weekend nights. For some low level social interaction with the other sex, what about a Friday night slow dance to live music with a neighborhood barfly thinking she is so chic and sophisticated smoking her slim feminine style cigarette while dancing under dimmed lighting. And seated at the bar a union worker still in his scuffed up work boots, unaware of the protocol of slow dancing, can't wait to cut in after he first downs a shot and a beer.

Then we have a regulation dart board at the end of the bar next to the men's room, which can lead to a drunken fist fight on a Saturday night when accusations are made about someone stepping over the line after they shoot triple corks.

Rico found his cigarettes, last one in the crumpled pack, groped around for his matches, found and used them, inhaled deeply, then he had this semi-cognizant moment while he glanced at everything around him. *I gotta get outta this dump. I just gotta. I need a fucking change in my life. I really fucking do.*

A what....?

A change in your life?

After you've been a jerk-off for most of your 29 years?

Everybody thinks you're nothing more than a not-too-bright smart-ass. You got kicked out of High School for failing grades and being disruptive in class. You almost got charged with assault going downtown to rough up some socialites at a trendy coffee house located close to up-scale Rittenhouse Square, only escaping the charges because you had a distant uncle who had some political connections.

Then there was the brawl on the union picket line at the trucking company on Aramingo Avenue making front page news.

Military service wanted no part of you when you tried to enlist when you were eighteen years old even though you told the military recruiter you wanted to "fuck up the enemy."

And here you are now set in place after 29 years, a fork lift operator on a loading dock at a chemical plant located in the Kensington section of the city working in a dead end job for low wages, and you're on the verge of blowing that.

A change…?

To what?

An astronaut floating around out there somewhere in deep space?

Then it hits him like a sucker punch to the gut while he's trying to work the problem about how he can both bring about a change his life and get out of this dump and into another place at the same monthly rent and maybe even in a better neighborhood.

What the hell happened with Arlene last night?

He wiped more sweat and grit from the back of his neck.

What was it she said?

Rico switched on a useless window fan good only for sucking in more factory dust and blasted heat.

What the hell does she want anyhow?

Still somewhat hung over from the night before, and his mind now being overworked due to the mental strain of trying to sort things out at the present moment, Rico wanted to let things go for a minute so he got up and went to the bathroom to take a piss so that he might also relieve himself from some of the alcohol he drank the night before.

Rico and Arlene have known each other since they were both seventeen. Arlene was the wholesome girl-next-door attractive at seventeen, and Rico introduced himself to her after he punched out some jerk-off who was pestering her at a neighborhood bus stop with some loud risqué sexual talk about how nice she was built.

First thoughts that hit Arlene after the jerk-off cowered down the street massaging his jaw wanting to make sure it still works: *Is this guy some kind of a hero or something along that line? And why would he do this for me? He is kind of good looking in a different kind of way."*

Rico held Arlene's hand momentarily.

He seemed concerned.

He asked if she was okay.

She nodded, getting herself together, and she nodded again.

He asked, "Maybe I'll see you around?"

She replied, almost smiling: "Maybe."

Arlene was smitten right there at the corner bus stop, watching Rico walk away, waiting for the Route J bus on her way to school and she knew she had seen him around the neighborhood always trying to act so cool and so tough. *I'm gonna have to try and hit on that girl if it's the last thing I do*, Rico thought to himself, glancing back at Arlene, also thinking his thoughts would make a great line in a hit song.

Arlene's parents operated a successful neighborhood corner grocery store and she grew up somewhat privileged, for this neighborhood at least. She attended a private school, and as she was an only child, her parents wanted only the best for her. Only the best for her did not include neighborhood smart ass, Rico Paradise, or anyone else of his kind. Educated, well mannered, having some prospects for the future were attributes Arlene was told she should be looking for in anyone she dated.

Arlene's parents were livid when Rico started coming around knocking on their door, obscured behind sunglasses, cigarette in hand, asking if he could see Arlene and maybe take her out on a date sometime.

The more Arlene's parents railed, the more she was drawn to Rico.

"He's not your kind. What in heaven's name is wrong with you? Would you please, please, listen to us!"

"There's good in him. I can see it," she tried telling her parents, who flatly refused to listen to anything she had to say.

Their first date behind her parents' back was a Saturday night double-feature at the Circle Theater on Frankford Avenue, then burgers and shakes at the *El Rancho Western Style Restaurant,* again on Frankford Avenue just above Wissinoming Park. At the ornate movie theater, with the swirling bright colored lights of the marquee giving off an aura of a carnival, they sat high up in the balcony, and all Rico wanted to do—he could care less about the movie—was make out with Arlene. Rico called it "serious lip locking."

During the second feature main attraction, Rico kept trying to get his hand up Arlene's summer dress. She resisted between deep kisses getting her all hot and bothered just reluctantly pushing his hand aside, while this biblical movie was playing which he took her to see thinking it would show her he had some religion about him and he was a decent guy with good morals and he had no wrong intent on his mind.

So much for religion and morals and good intent with his hand up her summer dress trying to go higher.

At the *El Rancho*, between sips on her milk-shake, while the juke box played a heart breaking top-ten hit song about teenage angst, Arlene asked Rico in a somewhat serious voice hoping to gain some insights about the guy seated in the same booth with her, "What do you want to do with your life?"

"That's a stupid damn question to ask me. That question makes no sense at all. What are you trying to get at?"

"No, I'm serious. Have you set any goals for yourself? Everybody sets some kind of goals for himself. We have to give ourselves some kind of direction. Don't we?"

Rico paused, a flustered look on his face, running the question through his head between deep drags on his cigarette. No one ever asked Rico questions like this before. "That's still a stupid question to ask me, but give me a second to think about it." Rico nervously tapped his fingertips on the table as if that body language might provide him with some answers to Arlene's questions. Thought process wise, he was distracted by the lyrics to the song playing on the juke box.

Rico gets back to Arlene's question.

"Sure I got goals. Doesn't anyone? I'll be

something or another. Who knows anything about this bullshit?"

Dancing suggestively close together and giving each other passionate kisses in front of the juke box playing the heart breaking teenage angst song, the restaurant manager hurries over telling the couple this is a family place and to it break it up and take it somewhere else. The manager unplugs the juke box, the song quick stopping and the lights flickering before going out.

Rico noticing the incident, mumbles something about the song being one of his favorites, and he continues.

"Who cares about it anyway?

I got plenty of time to sort things out.

What's....What's the rush?"

Finished taking Arlene's oral test, Rico shrugs his shoulders, slouches in the corner booth, and he looks across the table at Arlene now rummaging through her purse for change to help cover the tab.

Rushing out from the kitchen door, spurs on her cowgirl boots jingling as part of the required western styled uniform to fit the restaurant's motif, a waitress her tray balanced high aloft with burgers and shakes stops at the next booth. She lowers the tray setting it on the table, cracks chewing gum, and she asks, "Anything else?"

Arlene adds this, somewhat pressing the issue: "I think we should want to do something with our lives so we can say at some point in our life; I'm proud of myself. I really am."

Arlene set out goals for her life. Nothing profound; just the basics: Get a good education. Always do the right thing. Try to have a good life.

Trouble was, she kept getting stuck along the way.

Four months after their first date at the ornate *Circle Theater* and the *El Rancho Western Style Restaurant*, Rico and Arlene made slam-bam rock the springs steam up the windows serious lip locking back seat teenage love in Rico's old man's worn out Buick parked last row isolated at the drive-in movie just across the Tacony Bridge in Palmyra New Jersey. And somehow, maybe it was just by chance, or Rico didn't bother to check the newspaper ads, the same biblical movie was playing while Rico and Arlene were groaning in the back seat of a worn out Buick.

Arlene's parents weren't stupid.

They were both quite perceptive.

They knew something was going on and the

thought of it made them cringe. Devoting their life to Arlene, they weren't about to let someone like Rico Paradise ruin things. Arlene's father, after a Sunday morning church service, ran into Rico corner-hanging in the neighborhood. And he was trying to control his rising anger, and he was upset over the fact this situation was turning him into an angry person.

"Stay away from my daughter!"

He wanted to shake the living hell out of Rico.

"I'm damn warning you! Stay away! Pick someone else who's more like you."

Arlene's father always advised his daughter to try to surround herself with people who will bring you up and give you positive input and encouragement. Rico, he knew, was the direct opposite of this.

Finished taking a piss, Rico splashed warm sink water on his face, glanced at himself in the mirror, more splashed water, coughed three body wracking coughs, another glance in the mirror, and he asked himself a question. It was short. Only three words. It went like this:

"What the fuck....?"

He repeated himself before getting

somewhat cleansed and dressed.

"What the fuck....?"

Grabbing a fresh pack of cigarettes and some loose change from his bureau drawer, Rico left his apartment thinking about how he could straighten things out with Arlene, but he thought it might be best if he called her first instead of just showing up at her place.

At *Johnny Cee's Friendly Neighborhood Bar and Grille,* he turned left. Rico took a few steps and he looked back over his shoulder then having to shield his eyes from the glare of the directly overhead orange sun.

The roar of a silver passenger train streaking by over the black railroad bridge behind the power tool factory caught his attention. The silver passenger train was taking people who knows where. Maybe a cultural event in New York City, but most certainly, they weren't getting off anywhere around here.

From across the street, neighbor Ralph Lewis, on vacation from his plumber's job at the Philadelphia Navy Yard, waved to Rico.

Rico offered a weak response while quick stepping.

Ralph Lewis was packing his station wagon

being almost ready to take his wife and kids for a day trip down to the Jersey shore. A few houses across the street, including Ralph Lewis', displayed American flags and red, white, and blue patriotic bunting twisted around porch railings in celebration for the 4th of July weekend.

"Damn! Where is she?"

Walter Liteski's vision has understandably diminished under the strain after years and years of making certain the application from the physician's pen to the person in some sort of medical duress is accurate and precise. Liteski still proudly displays above his prescription measuring devices, framed, somewhat yellowed at the edges, Cum Laude degrees from an area Catholic university and a prestigious school of medicine located in Virginia.

Diminished vision aside, from the rear prescription filling area of his corner drug store, amid shelves of reference books and dark bottles filled to varying degrees with health-giving elixirs, Walter Liteski clearly saw the angry and confused look on Rico's face as he rushed in bringing with him commotion and waves of oppressive heat to the non-air-conditioned store.

Having no consideration whatsoever for the pharmacist's task at hand, Rico slammed the door shut with considerable force putting the "Yes We Are Open" hanging sign in a frantic side-to-side swinging motion. He dug in his pockets fumbling for some change, gave off agitated body signals, and he mumbled something towards Liteski about having to make an important call and he would have made it at his apartment but the telephone company screwed up his bill and cut off his service.

Not him again! I'm tired of his nonsense. Damn, just get the hell out of here! Liteski grimaced to himself, totally ignoring Rico with a look of contempt.

Located alongside a neighborhood mom-and-pop card and gift shop, and across the street from a nondescript-looking church constructed with earthen colored bricks, Liteski's corner drug store has as a communication point a dated single person telephone booth with a folding glass door, a shelf possibly in place for change calculation or note taking during conversation, and a view of the intersection of Margaret and Melrose Streets in the Frankford section of the city.

Just finishing up a vial of soon to be picked up antibiotic, and about to affix the correct dosage label, the druggist's concentration was again distracted by the slamming of the folding glass door to the telephone booth, done seemingly with the intent to cause structural damage to the front of the store.

Rico slammed himself down on the telephone booth seat in the same motion tossing some change on the shelf for calculation. And in his disturbed frame of mind as far as what's going on with Arlene, he had to pause and think about her telephone number instead of just dialing it from memory.

Inserting the correct change, Rico then dialed, shook a cigarette from his fresh pack, used his matches, inhaled deeply on the filtered cigarette, impatiently tapped window glass, and waited for Arlene to pick up. Just then, Rico didn't hear them, the church bells rang out from across the street; as they always do precisely at twelve in the afternoon and at six in the evening.

Rico had no idea as to what he was going to say to Arlene outside of just running his mouth off which was his way of dealing with her whenever things got messed up.

Five rings. "Pick up! Pick up!"

Agitated, he flicks coins around on the

telephone booth shelf.

Seven rings. "Come on! Come on!"

More impatient tapping on window glass and the church bells stop ringing.

Ten rings. "Damn! Where is she?"

Already sixty plus hours into a long and tiresome week accomplished without help, his wife is ill and unable to help out, and two sons and a daughter with indifferences towards the family business are doing things in other states, Liteski was far removed from wanting to put up with any kind of nonsense from the neighborhood pain in the ass in his telephone booth.

Thoughts of just selling the business and getting out have been running through his mind more and more after years of too many demanding hours and having to listen to old people constantly moaning and complaining about their various and never-ending ailments and illnesses. He has been carrying this worn out feeling for quite some time even though the store has provided him with an income level far above the average. Looking back regretfully now for allowing himself years ago to be pressured into continuing the family business instead of pursuing the dreams of his youth, Liteski the neighborhood pharmacist lowered what has

over the years taken the rough edges off the day –
a red plastic Emerson radio now playing Perry
Como moaning a dreary love song that could put
most people into a deep sleep.

Six more unanswered rings and Rico's
anger turned physical slamming the receiver into
the telephone apparatus with such force if the
telephone booth were free standing instead of
being securely attached to the corner drug store, it
would have tilted askew in double-digit degrees.

Reluctantly, confrontation being the last
thing on his mind, Liteski went around the
prescription counter, he inched alongside the
cosmetic and fragrance section to investigate the
commotion at the same time hoping for some
customers to come in thinking their presence would
prevent Rico from causing any kind of a scene.

The store seemed hotter.

Two whirling fans on metal stands and
outdoor green canvas window awnings
accomplished nothing cooling-wise.

For the moment, it was even quieter, no
more Perry Como moaning a dreary love song on a
red plastic Emerson radio.

Reserved, respected, and well-liked in the
neighborhood, Walter Liteski was beyond weary of

Rico's simple minded antics. Was beyond weary of his risqué jokes.

"Did you hear the one about....?"

Was beyond weary of the "Wanna flip double or nothing?" game he would constantly try to goad Liteski into playing on cigarette and breath mint purchases he made, knowing full damn well he was getting under the druggist's skin with his simple-minded games.

And now this. On a damn hot July Saturday in the year 1985, and the druggist was ten years shy of full retirement.

"Just get the hell out and stay the hell out! Take your damn business somewhere else! I'm sick and tired of your damn nonsense!" Liteski was ready to explode the words as soon as the door to the telephone booth opened fully.

Always known to speak in a low voice, and for conducting himself in a professional manner, the rising anger Liteski was feeling was going against his grain and he didn't want to alarm his wife who was resting in their second floor living quarters.

After first retrieving his refunded telephone change, then grabbing his leftover change and cigarettes, Rico opened the door half way then pausing noticing his matches still on the shelf, and

Liteski was an instant away from spewing out his words when the door fully opened.

Catching Liteski's attention, the front door opens without the open or closed sign in any side to side motion. And more reassuring than a few customers walking in at the same time, wiping sweat from his brow with the sleeve of his uniform shirt, in walks the neighborhood police officer on patrol stopping by to sign the police log book.

"How's things? Damn hot out there it is."

The cop shuts the door and takes two steps inside.

"Mind if I get a drink from your water cooler?"

The appearance and questions from the officer breaking the tension and the druggist feeling this welcomed sense of relief. "Sure, go ahead. It's back there," he replies, pointing.

"Everything okay?" The officer asks, still two steps inside the front door, glancing around, having a gut feeling that something's wrong.

Rico fully opens the door.

"You don't look all that well. You seem upset....Are you?" the officer asks Liteski just as Rico steps out from the telephone booth.

Startled, one thought hits Rico real quick.

He tells himself he had better calm the hell down right away because he recognizes the officer knowing he got hurt trying to break up the brawl at the union picket line at the trucking company on Aramingo Avenue some three years ago. Two cops got hurt, and three union drivers, Rico included, lost their jobs. Rico knows damn right well the cop is just waiting for him to step out of line so he can run him the hell in for a trip down to the Roundhouse.

Slowly getting his words out in a low monotone fashion, Rico excuses himself.

He side steps around the officer.

The officer refreshes his memory to himself: *I know this fucking guy! He was a big man on the picket line a few years back screaming and yelling with all of his union buddies there to back him up.*

Rico opens the door, leaves, and closes the door the reverse of the way he came in. Two minutes pass and he doesn't notice the sign being switched to the: "Sorry, We're Closed" position.

So there's Rico outside the corner drug store under a high up orange sun leaning against an olive green postal mail box, taking deep drags on his cigarette, perspiring in the July heat without having anything on his person to wipe away sweat and grit. He's all twisted up on the inside and

31

angrily he flicks his cigarette butt to the pavement and crushes it with the heel of his almost worn out pointed-toe black dress shoe. And if you saw him there, under the high up orange sun, leaning against a postal mail box, you could tell just by looking at him that something was really wrong with him. But you wouldn't think of asking him if he was okay because he would probably tell you to get fucked.

Tilted slightly to one side giving off acrid fumes, a Route J bus rumbles by all of the windows opened wide, passengers inside with wilted expressions on their faces, the bus driver wearing thick sunglasses and a sweat stained uniform cap with a black sun visor. Rico thinks even though the bus is in motion, it's probably just as hot as his apartment.

Three-hundred-pound Chuffy Howell drives by behind the Route J bus squeezed into his sleek European sport's convertible. He waves to Rico, then he speeds up, not even thinking about offering Rico a ride.

Ten minutes pass and the overhead sun is still relentless.

He lights another cigarette, thinking, perspiring even more.

Rico's thoughts get interrupted abruptly; the officer getting right up in his face warning him if he bothers the druggist one more time he'll have some real problems to deal with. The cop has this *go ahead and try me* scowl on his face.

Rico nods in acknowledgement, not wanting to risk getting jacked up right there on the corner. Now the officer knew he couldn't do anything to Rico just because he slammed some doors in a corner drug store on a hot July Saturday, but Rico's response to his warning told the officer everything he needed to know should a one-on-one situation ever arise in the future.

For close to twelve years, Rico and Arlene have had this in-and-out of each other's life, revolving door thing going on. Once three years went by and they didn't speak. Arlene was once engaged to a carpenter who was in business for himself, but after a year she broke it off without giving any explanations why. The carpenter really loved Arlene, and he was reconditioning a run-down house they planned to live in after they were married.

Then Rico and Arlene were back together in the same revolving door way they connected with each other seemingly picking up where they left off.

They will both tell you they have always felt this bond, this connection to each other. But it's always been on and off, like some kind of a switch-click, click, click.

In the on position, things were real good.

Switch turned off: It's like they went down roaring in flames.

Lately though, Arlene wanted more.

She wanted a chance for something. To live her life with someone.

Friends and family would ask, "Why do you bother with him?"

She would reply, "Things will work out. There's good in him."

Her best friend, Sally, would plead, "Run!... Run from that man as fast as you can! You don't need someone like him in your life!"

Rico walked back over Margaret Street.

He's thinking he should go over to Arlene's place on Bermuda Street to see how things stand.

He knows it's all about last night.

He doesn't know this. Arlene's not there. She's had enough.

A sense of obligation.

So here's Rico the night before playing cards in Chuffy Howell's basement on Tacony Street just a block away from the soon-to-be-closed and boarded up Henry Wadsworth Longfellow Elementary School. Outside at midnight, it's still a sultry 85 degrees. Inside, Chuffy provided niceties: cheap beer on ice in a laundry tub, cold cuts and rolls, greasy chips and napkins, a bottle or two of hard liquor for the regulars only, and of course a cooling system. Yeah sure—a squeaky window fan wedged into a basement window which years ago accepted a coal truck's chute.

Chuffy Howell's was the elite card playing gig in the area. They came from South Philly to the Greater Northeast. From Manayunk to Port Richmond. Chuffy's dad, *Pork Chops* – that's damn right, *Pork Chops*! – do you think these names are made up? Well they're not, and it's a neighborhood thing of tradition. Just about everyone went by some unique moniker drawn from some colorful incident in his life.

The *Pork Chop's* incident briefly defined: Years ago, during a cold brutal winter, things were slow on the docks for Chuffy's dad. He did have his pride and wanted to provide his family with a special holiday dinner with all the trimmings. So he goes food shopping without adequate funding. He tries to walk through the supermarket doors with two packs of *Pork Chops* stuffed in his coat pockets with the manager and two cashiers in hot pursuit. The judge was lenient. He actually chuckled, saying his courtroom could use an influx of humor. Said the judge, then sternly looking down on the defendant, "If you ever come before me again, *Pork Chops*, you'll do jail time."

And the name stuck.

Anyhow. *Pork Chops* started the game some fifteen years ago to avoid spending any quality weekend time with his overweight and argumentative wife. Chuffy has proudly taken over for his dad, a family lineage thing with the father still there to give advice and counsel and work the game part-time just in case any trouble breaks out.

The gambling could at times last the weekend, with a Sunday morning break for religious services for those so inclined. Generally, only the losers went, saying prayers for a change in their luck hoping to get some of their money back in the afternoon session so they could avoid dealing with a loan shark who could have you busted up for nonpayment of funds borrowed.

Chuffy and Dad's neighborhood card game

in their row house basement after fifteen years had a cast of characters, some shady and non-talkative, coming and going. Some of them, you certainly didn't want to play with. Somehow though, somehow, the police never raided the place. That's damn strange and unusual considering all the people, most of them being the unsavory kind, traipsing in and out at all hours of the day and night. Maybe Chuffy and *Pork Chops* greased some palms over the years to keep the cops from breaking down their door and dragging them out handcuffed and all.

You think?

All those years and not one raid; come on now!

The house rules: Dealer's choice as long as you called draw poker, five or seven card stud, or three card andy.

The finance rules: It depended on who was playing, it could fluctuate based on the cash around the table. Basically the game started out at a buck in, two bucks to open, a three buck betting limit, but you could raise what you put in the pot, and it went on from there—with Chuffy taking a cut from every pot—to pay for the niceties, of course.

One other finance rule strictly enforced with

no exceptions: No borrowing from another player or from Chuffy himself should you go broke. "I'm not running a bank here! No fucking loans!" Chuffy was sure to exclaim to everyone, his 300-pound union-organizing frame telling everyone he means it. Chuffy Howell made some big bucks cutting pots.

Want some proof? Parked out back in the rear driveway, his status symbol: A sleek low slung shiny black European sport's car with a maroon foxtail tied to the radio antenna. *Pork Chops*, too, had a little one-bedroom (get-away from his overweight wife) trailer he was paying off, parked down at the Jersey shore just as you drive into Wildwood Crest.

So risking house and food money, car and rent payments, money for shoes and clothes for the kids, for some their life savings rolled up in a wad of bills, and even putting your marriage at risk, there's six guys seated at an old kitchen table inlaid with fake marble. And there's five guys standing around the table just waiting for the chance to try their luck. There's profanity exclaimed with emphasis, players downing shots of hard liquor attempting to settle their nerves, bluffing and finger pointing, a cough producing cigarette haze, the cooling system blowing in sticky night air, 300-pound Chuffy Howell eyeballing the pot speed munching on a liverwurst and onion sandwich, and Raysel, the *Neighborhood Bookie*, is cursing his luck throwing his cards down in utter disgust.

"Son of a bitch! What the fuck's going on here?"

Raysel the *Neighborhood Bookie* had the distinguished looks of a college professor who taught advanced science courses at institutions where only students of the highest intellect and financial backing were welcomed. But if things went wrong for Raysel, like losing at cards at Chuffy Howell's, or if you fucked with him by not paying off a bet in proper time, he could get real nasty.

Rico was having one of those runs when everything just goes right, and he could do no wrong, and everything he tried turns golden. He was torching Raysel, the *Neighborhood Bookie*, on just about every hand, or at least it seemed that way.

Raysel has two pairs. Rico's two pairs are higher.

Raysel draws three jacks. Rico squeezes in a third king.

Raysel pulls a straight. Rico gets a flush.

So screwed up was Raysel's thought

process from his bad luck, he even let Rico bluff him out of a winning hand.

"Damn! This is fun. Damn, I like this; you know, getting even with you for once." Rico exclaimed sarcastically, breaking Raysel's balls, downing a shot of Chuffy's liquor, then wiping his mouth with the back of his hand somewhat laughing pointing towards Raysel holding him up to ridicule in front of the players at the table and those standing around it.

Pissed off, Raysel shot back, "Play fucking cards! Cut the bullshit!"

"All right! It's your deal," Rico replied, pushing the cards towards Raysel, smirking, then adding, "You took enough money off me over the years. You had your claws into me. Remember the threats? Just call this payback. Now call your game!"

Trying to break the building tension in Chuffy Howell's basement, Johnny Rat, standing behind Rico, swigged canned beer, then asked out loud, "Did anyone hear about the jerk-off Shumaker kid? The one with the bulldog tattooed on his arm?" Now this is a story in itself. Richie Shumaker, about eighteen years old and without gainful employment, found out last week to his great surprise that his girlfriend might be knocked up.

Richie's thought process was all twisted up. He didn't know what to do as far as getting a marriage license or looking for an apartment. He didn't have any insurance for needed medical attention or any money for child support. His father told him, "You screwed up! You deal with it! It's your problem. And don't bother me with it!"

So Richie figures out the best way to deal with the situation is to join the military service of his choice and get as far away from the problem as he can. So Richie packs some things and he goes to the neighborhood military recruitment office and he announces to the person in charge seated at the desk while holding a military salute he saw on a television war movie, "I wanna join up. I wanna shoot down enemy aircraft, and I'm ready to leave right now." With that said, Richie cuts off the salute he saw on television and he attempts to stand at the military position of attention.

His uniform nicely starched, and adorned with medals awarded after years of combat service in all of the troubled spots in the world, the recruitment sergeant looks up from his paperwork and he thinks to himself, *After all these years! After all I've seen! Why fucking me?*

Now the recruitment sergeant was all military and he wanted to follow the correct procedure mandated whenever a situation like this comes up. The procedure being exactly what to do should a screwball come in wanting to enlist. He walks around his desk. He puts his arm on Richie's shoulder, and escorts him to the front door. And he says to Richie in a voice only the two of them could hear, "Get the hell out of here, and don't ever come back."

Later that night, Richie's hanging on the corner with the other guys bullshitting them, bragging he is going away for military service and he will be shooting down enemy airplanes after a few weeks of useless basic training.

After downing two quart-bottles of beer he swiped from his old man and smoking a couple of joints, he tells everyone, "It's too damn hot. I can't think straight with this heat. I gotta take a swim." Richie staggers off towards the playground situated about three-hundred feet west of the railroad tracks behind the power tool factory. He scales a brick wall, strips naked, and he swan dives into the deep end of the pool.

Like he really needed this with all he's faced with. Richie didn't know they closed and drained the pool earlier in the day due to a high urine count. They found Richie fucked up at the bottom of the pool somewhere between unconscious and half-dead. He came out of this pretty much okay considering what he went through. The medical team did, however, have to do an install job, inserting a steel plate on the top of his head. One thing though, if you made eyeball-to-eyeball contact with Richie, he had this distant faraway look in his eyes. Like the lights are on but nobody's home.

"Call your game!" Rico repeats, glaring, holding Raysel up for more ridicule in front of everyone else. "And the hell with the stupid Shumaker kid."

Rico played his own brand of poker which was against all the conventional poker playing theories known at that time. He chased two-card flushes and inside straights. He thought two low pairs were big. And he thought he would always catch trips on high pairs squinting at you from over the top of his cards trying to squeeze the third one in. Tonight the unconventional became theory, like Einstein at a blackboard chalk in hand explaining $E=mc^2$. As if anybody could understand Einstein explaining $E=mc^2$.

And why the hell didn't Raysel just change

the game when it was his deal instead of trying to beat Rico at his own game?

Try five card stud!

Try seven card stud!

Try three card andy!

It's only logical.

Really, if you go outside and get hit by a bus. Next time, try something different. Go out the back door. Again, it's only logical.

By one in the morning, Raysel the *Bookie* was just about wiped out financially. He was pissed off and about ready to explode. The rent was due on Monday and he was a month behind. And his wife was breaking his stones hounding him about the twins needing dental braces. Raysel came with the most money, a good part of it being numbers bets he didn't turn in yet. And heaven help Raysell should someone hit a number and the betting slips weren't turned in.

Troubles. Troubles. Troubles.

Sometimes life throws you some curves. Rico cleaned Raysel out big time with his uncanny, against all the rules luck. The ball breaker: Rico drew two hearts for a flush beating Raysel's three kings for an eighty dollar pot. Holding his head in his hands, almost sick to his stomach, looking down on Rico's winning hand in utter disbelief, with a slightly trembling hand Raysell flung his losing cards on the concrete basement floor, scratching them up, pissing Chuffy off.

"Read 'em, and weep!" Rico added, breaking balls.

The four other players:

Ronnie the *Big Cad*, who ran a car crushing business.

Johnny Gonsho, a former boxer, who took a dive or two.

Sal the *Blade*, from South Philly (A.K.A. The Lounge Lizard).

And Sonka the *Tailor*, who managed a custom shirt shop downtown patronized by mob figures, just shook their heads collectively grateful they weren't second best to Rico's scorching luck.

Know what it's like being second best at cards? Expensive! Damn expensive! Standing around the table, first cousins and postal mailman, Stubby and Skull Stukowski, both exclaimed they were glad they weren't sitting in right now playing against Rico's scorching luck.

Chuffy Howell was in a neutral mode, grinning this greedy grin, not caring who won or lost taking another cut from the pot with his short and stubby fat hands, his pinkie finger flaunting a gaudy extra-large size cat's eye ring.

Maybe a much larger size convertible next, huh Chuffy?

Something that you don't have to lubricate yourself to get inside.

What a time, around twenty-after-one, to have a sense of obligation thing hit Rico when considering the streak he has going. Although he does have enough down payment cash right now to somewhat upscale his life by getting a better apartment in a nicer neighborhood and having his telephone service reconnected. He even passes up a shot of hard liquor offered as a congratulatory gesture from Chuffy Howell in tribute to his great night.

"Wow! I've never seen a streak of luck like this before," Chuffy exclaimed, then downing the shot of liquor himself.

Seething, Raysel the *Bookie* tells Chuffy to "get fucked!"

Things have been going pretty good with Arlene lately, and Rico promised to pick her up from her part-time waitress job at the *Lit Club* on Melrose Street, just down the street from the nondescript-looking church on the corner. Besides any sense of obligation, he has other motives. Rico has a high state of arousal going on around his zipper area and he needs more than a quick feel job from Arlene so he can release his mounting sexual tension.

He's thinking to himself.

It's been a little while.

Got a case of the horns pretty bad.

Rico also figures out he has rode the winning streak long enough and with Raysel just about broke, now is a good time to go (it was personal now) leaving Raysel all screwed up.

Catching everyone by complete surprise, especially Raysel, Rico announced hurriedly getting up from his chair moving it back in the same motion causing scrapping sounds on the concrete floor. "Well guys, that's it for me tonight. Gotta run! Catch you later! Remember, the sun always shines on those who wait. Remember that! You guys will get another shot at me." Rico's words coming out and falling down especially on Raysel.

While Rico was stuffing his pockets with his winnings, including Raysell's rent money and the money backing numbers bets he didn't turn in, this time bomb was set to go off. Now totally pissed off and just about broke outside of a few dollars, just enough for a hand or two, and over the edge panicking over what he was going to tell his wife, Raysell shot back in a voice that went clean through the basement window fan and down Tacony Street.

"You gonna quit like this!?"

"Damn it! Gimme a chance to get something back!"

"Whadda you do, win and run? You're a real prick; you know that!"

An even-voiced reply, "Like I said; I gotta run. Understand?"

Forty-year-old Raysel went nuts. "You're a real jerk-off; you know that!" Raysel shouted back, finger-pointing, his face an angry shade of red, spraying beer soaked saliva, neck veins pulsating getting up from his chair showing he was going to step up to Rico.

"You wanna take this outside Raysel? Do you really? I'll kick the living hell out of you! Go ahead, fuck with me!"

It was a tense, tense moment in the neighborhood.

"Go ahead and try me! See what happens!" Rico added, his voice enraged, and at the same time calm, ready to go at it with Raysel right now.

Sonka the *Tailor* just looked down at the table, eyes riveted, trying to find outlines of faces in the fake marble, not wanting Rico to get all in his face. Ronnie the *Big Cad*, and Johnny Gonsho were staying out of it, not even wanting to try to remedy the situation. Besides, they didn't lose anything compared to what Raysel lost.

Chuffy gagged on liverwurst and onion.

Hearing the fracas, *Pork Chops* flew down the steps breaking off bickering with his wife about his penchant for spending alleged solitary time in his trailer in the Crest while his wife had to fill her time with her brother and sister, Stosh and Stella, on Stiles Street. Time drags ever so slowly when things are on the verge of going ballistic.

Pork Chops and Son, entrepreneurs of this sucking off winners and losers alike card game, were both close to a state of panic should this situation escalate outside and the cops come, sirens wailing, and bust the game and lock everyone up.

No more sleek convertibles for Chuffy.

No more part-time bucks; no more get away trailer at the Crest. So *Pork Chops* might get the chance to bond a little more with his argumentative and overweight wife on weekends.

49

Seconds pass, Johnny Rat suppresses a cough.

Pork Chops thinks he hears police sirens wailing in the distance.

Someone standing around the table reluctantly offered stuttering words trying to defuse the situation. "Stay the hell out of this!" Rico responded, glaring at Raysel.

Raysel then has some will to survive, *I don't want to get myself busted up*, second thoughts running through his head; his bravado wearing off. He doesn't think he'll come out too good in an all-out brawl with Rico, knowing at times he can be half to three quarters crazy.

So, washed in both fear and common sense, Raysel blinked first.

Then ever so slowly he eased himself back on his chair everyone else now looking at him in a non-fearing light. Now Rico had his flaws, his kinks, but here now in a calmer Tacony Street basement, he shook *Pork Chop's* hand treating him like a well-respected man. He offered an apology, and just like that he was up the steps and gone.

Sal the *Blade* swigged canned beer, belched, and asked, "Is it the *Big Cad*'s deal?" Johnny Rat brazenly stated, wanting to sit in Rico's lucky spot, "I'm taking Rico's place!"

No one spoke to Raysel. He sat there shaken, almost unable to move.

A crisis averted, Chuffy Howell cried out: "Drinks for everyone! On the house!"

"Marry someone who loves you."

Wailing police sirens *Pork Chops* thinks he heard seem closer now. Rico's standing outside Chuffy's row house under illuminating street lights counting and straightening out crumpled bills in the sultry heat, the sirens suddenly alarming him and interfering with his concentration. The last damn thing Rico needed was cops pulling up and recognizing him, then frisking him finding the wad of bills, then pressuring him as far as how he obtained so much cash, and the answer is right there looking down through Chuffy's basement window. All Rico needed was the police busting the game up on his account then him having to face the wrath of Chuffy and *Pork Chops* and everybody else who got locked up

Rico splits over a darkened side street, the sirens fading out in the distance, maybe going towards the decrepit housing projects behind the

Whitehall Commons Playground. The same playground where Richie Shumaker took a swan dive into the deep end of an empty pool.

Pausing in front of the *Sueffert Soda Bottling Works*, Rico takes a few calming deep breaths before popping in some black Sen-Sen pellets trying to scrape away the alcohol and cigarette taste in his mouth. Rico tries to compose himself from the high drama of the past twenty minutes or so. The rush of the almost-brawl with Raysel the *Bookie* has a slight sobering effect on him. He straightens himself out somewhat, tucking in his midnight blue Ban-Lon shirt, and he heads over Melrose Street towards the *Lit Club*, and Arlene, in the 4600 block of Melrose Street.

His mind races sexual in thought with his quick steps.

Hope I get lucky with Arlene tonight. It's been a while.

Meet Rico James Paradise: Deep thinker on intimacy.

He passes *Old Lady Canary's* middle of the block shoe-box-sized convenience store.

Hope she lets me stay over.

Damn work tomorrow!

Six A. M. comes up quick.

Passing trees lining the nondescript church with heat lightening rumbling towards the west, over the Frankford El, Rico spits out Sen-Sen then lighting his next-to-last cigarette and he rushes up six steps and rings the doorbell at the *Lit Club*. Half a minute passes, a second ring, "Come on! Open up!" Then a hand pushes aside a small window curtain. Bartender Bobby Cee peers through door glass. He nods in recognition, then unlocking the door letting Rico in.

"Thanks Bobby. Where's Arlene?" He asked, stepping inside the narrow club carved out from side-by-side row houses. Wanting to look at least half decent for Arlene, Rico runs a pocket comb through his hair checking out his reflection in door glass. Rico imagines he sees an image of James Dean reflecting back at him.

"She's almost on her way out," Bobby Cee replied gesturing right handed towards Arlene, who was straightening tables and chairs at the far end of the bar.

A few more steps inside at the cigarette machine, he asks, "Hey baby! Almost ready? Getting late you know."

"Just a few minutes. I'm almost done. You're a little early."

Bobby Cee flicked off most of the ceiling lights then going behind the bar sponging away liquor stains and cigarette ash, some left by old men with trembling hands. His work night just about over, Bobby Cee finished it off with three fingers of vodka in a tall glass.

"Want any of this? Top shelf stuff.... Boss ain't here," he asked, holding the bottle slightly aloft, his voice raspy from too many unfiltered cigarettes. Rico waved him off, offering thanks. Sexed up, Rico waited in front of the bar, impatient, slouched on a bar stool, some remaining lights still on reflecting off liquor bottles on glass shelves behind the bar.

Bobby Cee had the hots for Arlene. He had the hots for her for some time. He'd really like to have a shot at her between the sheets, but he knew he better never let Rico find out.

Some whispered risqué sexual talk between the two, then questions:

"Did ya come from Chuffy's?"

"Yeah. After the race track."

"How'd you do?" Bobby Cee asked, picking tobacco from his teeth with the edge of a matchbook cover.

"Where?"

"At Chuffy's place"

"I cleaned Raysel the fuck out. And it's about time I got back at that prick," Rico replied in a low voice, leaning over a now clean bar, not wanting Arlene to hear his vile street talk.

"You better watch out for Raysel. He doesn't like losing. He might try to get even in some way."

Rico ignored the advice, knowing he left Raysel screwed up in more ways than one. Rico turned around, his back leaning against the bar, and Bobby Cee eyeballed Arlene real quick (she could sense it) then saying, "That's it for me. I'm gonna catch up with my brother Johnny over at his place. 'Hey Arlene! Would you close up?"

Arlene couldn't stand Bobby Cee. She could sense his eyes, always leering. "Sure. Go ahead."

"See you later Rico. You're a lucky guy to be with Arlene."

"Thanks Bobby. Somebody has to be lucky once in a while."

Rico's figuring-things-out mind went to work. "Gotta get outta here pretty soon if I hope to score and get some sleep before work."

He shifted his position on the barstool.

"Whadda you say Arlene? Gettin' late...." Rico asked, sexed up even more, thinking to himself, *she really looks good tonight.*

"Okay. Give me a minute or two."

She wiped tables clean while blowing out some candles and leaving a few lit. Then something happened that never happened before in all the times Rico came to see Arlene home from her part-time waitress job at the *Lit Club*.

Unplanned, or maybe it was, only she knows, it just somehow happened. Picture a scene from a 1940's genre movie with the leading lady debating with herself in a foggy airport whether she should just get on the propeller-driven airplane leaving behind the handsome leading man with the slicked back hair. Arlene appeared lost in thought at the far end of the bar finished straightening out tables and chairs.

"Arlene! Arlene......let's...." Trying to snap her out of it, the man's even more impatient now.

If Arlene was the leading lady in the 1940's genre movie done in black and white, she wasn't getting on the propeller-driven airplane.

With bright red selection buttons stretched out like keys on a piano, the ornate juke box has been in the same corner, to the left of the dart board, for as long as anyone could remember. Stroking aside a wisp of her blond hair, Arlene regained herself. She went over, resting her hand on dimly lit glass.

"Arlene!"

She paused, looking at the selections, and played B-17, some static the record needle searching for the groove.

"Arlene! What are you doing? Don't play that now! Let's go!" his words agitated, realizing it might delay him longer to get what he wants.

Now Rico comes over to pick Arlene up at the *Lit Club* feeling all amorous and turned on. And you would think he might feed her at least one of these lines to set the tone for the rest of the night.

"Hey baby, you really look good tonight."

"I've had you on my mind all day."

"I really want to be with you tonight."

"I can't wait to get you alone."

A mood change, just small right now, but somehow you could sense it. Not Rico though, still slouched, having nothing amorous to say.

Damn guy! Say something to make her feel special.

The recording needle finding the groove, one of the great love songs, The Flamingos: "I See Only You Forever." A love song you should live at least once in your life, having someone who loves you and they see no one else but you.

Dance real close to someone you love to this song.

Be intimate with someone you love to this song.

"I need you now and forever ..."

Words and a haunting melody that just take you out now mingling with light given off by a few flickering candles and a shadowy cigarette haze in the dimly lit empty club, save for two people, at two in the morning.

"Please listen, hear my plea...."

Arlene came within arm's reach of Rico, and she looked at him as if he was the most special man anywhere. Then this woman's touch, her fingertips just brushing his hand, ever so slightly; it makes most men feel glad they're men. If her best friend Sally was there at that precise moment, she would have cried out, "Are you blind?" Then using physical force if necessary pulling Arlene away imploring her to, "Run!...run away from this man as fast as you can! You don't need someone like him in your life."

"Take me in your arms, hold me close..."

"Would you dance with me?" She asked, taking his hand in her own, her voice just above a whisper.

"Arlene...It's..." He stammered, straightening himself somewhat, still thinking one thought.

"Dance with me... Please.....Hold me close," cutting him off in mid-sentence. "Come into my arms. You know I love you."

"A stolen kiss, taken from my lips, in the night...."

She took him half way into her arms. His mind not having caught up with the moment, Rico slow reacted, placing his arms loosely around her, hardly returning any feelings whatsoever; probably not even having any idea in him as far as how to return the feeling.

"Just listen to the words....Just listen." Her words soft, bringing him closer. "I feel these words. for you."

She pauses, "I really do."

Somehow, a slight awakening. Through everything else: The long night starting out at the race track. Too many beers and some shots of hard liquor. An almost brawl with Raysel the *Bookie* at Chuffy Howell's. What he really came here for, and even the love song; a feeling started to run through Rico. He felt a woman's touch like never before. Arlene caressed the back of his neck. She placed her arm tight around his waist.

Unplanned, or maybe not, perhaps now is just the time; it just happened. A quarter and B-17, and the Flamingos singing a love song coming from a dated juke box with bright red selection buttons. The two alone, two midnight people on distant far away edges, slow dancing now cheek-to-cheek in front of a now clean mahogany bar in a closed private club on Melrose street with daylight still hours away.

"Within your embrace, let this moment never end…"

Rico could feel Arlene pressed close.

Could feel her skin against his face.

Could feel a woman's caress like never before. Could feel deep inside himself feelings he never felt before.

He felt himself losing his center second by second. And you know all he came here for was the hope to get his rocks off with Arlene, sleep off a jag at her place, and make work in the morning at the chemical plant in the blue collar Kensington section of the city.

And now this, slow dancing cheek-to-cheek with the woman who loves him; probably the most intimate moment he ever had with a woman in his life. This not the way he was accustomed to doing things with the women in his life.

"....And I see only you forever."

The love song ended, and this silence, a silence you could hear. And the woman still holding fast, not letting go. It was a moment. Have you ever been there? Holding someone you love so close never wanting to let go.

Do you remember?

Would you go back to the moment if you could?

The side of her face on his shoulder, her feelings came out.

Rivers and rivers of them.

Emotional rivers after years and years of the in-and-out of each other's life-revolving-door-way they connected with each other. Emotional rivers of wanting a chance for something with the man she loved.

"It's been years for us now. Please tell me what you're feeling."

"What do you want? I don't want to keep going on like this."

"I just can't....Please, I can't."

"I need something more in my life."

The man's all dry mouthed now. He could

61

hardly get a word out.

He's losing his center even more. The room seemed tilted to him.

Should he stay? Does he even realize what's taking place here?

He has a chance for something.

Should he go running from the moment out into the sultry night?

Rico was out of kilter, his face expressionless. His hands dropped to his waist, then half-heartedly finding their way around Arlene again. So there's Rico half-holding the only woman who ever loved him in his 29 years, and his emotions just took flight leaving him a vacant man with, *I don't need this* thoughts running through him.

Then a question most men ask, now left for Arlene.

The words just came out. She doesn't even know where they came from. She thought someone else was speaking the words and she was another person standing stage right watching the scene evolve.

"Would you marry me?"

Arlene's mind raced realizing the words were said.

"Please! Please say yes! Or at least you will think about it, but for god sakes, don't say no. For god sakes, please don't say no!"

Rico hears something, swirling, hissing, from in front of him or behind him, off to the side, he's not sure. He looks around. Maybe the song playing again. Or voices trying to get through to him. *Arlene said something but it couldn't be that. Marriage? Why do I need that?*

Waiting for Rico to say something, anything, Arlene went on, her voice filled with emotion, flickering candles on the verge of going out.

"Marry someone who loves you."

"You can't live without love in your life."

"You just can't."

"With love in your life you can do great things."

Rico just stood there an empty man not even understanding what happened. And the voices came through. The voices of all men who came up small in moments like this when they had a chance for something. Hissing at Rico in the nearly dark private club: *Say something! Say something damn it! Don't just stand there! Look at the woman in front of you! Don't you realize what's going on here? This could be your chance for something. Don't wind up like us. Damn you...!*

The man heard nothing.

He stood there silent. His silence spoke volumes.

Great life trip so far for Rico James Paradise.

Before stepping away from Rico's arms holding her only half-heartedly, she told him this: "My heart is broken."

There was no anger in her, not even hurt, just this empty feeling. She came to fully realize at that moment they were just two people on distant far away edges.

With a tear sliding down her face, Arlene knew this: It's a damn heartache to have this happen. She loved him until her arms broke.

Arlene said a quick good night outside the *Lit Club,* adding she wanted to be alone and would be okay walking home by herself. For whatever the reason, she took his hand one last time. She kissed his cheek, then turned and walked away.

Rico just watched the woman who loved him walk away down Melrose Street. Like a fool he just watched her walk away. He couldn't see the tears sliding down her face. Night voices cried out: *Go after her! Damn you; go after her! You damn fool! Don't let her walk away.*

Rico only heard heat lightening rumbling towards the west, over the Frankford El. Arlene turned the corner at the appliance store at Bermuda Street. Rico mouthed something to himself, but it's too late now. The deed is done. He should have said it sooner: "I love you Arlene."

He had a great life after watching the woman who loved him walk out of his life down Melrose Street. He had the race track, the corner bars, and the card games at Chuffy Howell's, including friends Ronnie the *Big Cad*, Johnny Gonsho and Sonka the *Tailor*. He even had Friday night slow dances with a neighborhood hussy at *Johnny Cee's Friendly Neighborhood Bar and Grille.* Rico even got a better job and an apartment in a little nicer neighborhood.

There were times late at night when Rico would end his day by himself in a rundown corner bar and he would think back and reality would hit. He would tell himself this isn't the way to live and he really screwed things up. And maybe just by chance someone would play the B-17 song and somehow he could feel her presence. Startled, he would look around, over his shoulder, hoping she was there ("god please be there!") asking him to come into her arms and hold her close. Turning back around feeling so damn empty finishing his drink, hearing the bartender announce "last call," he remembered her words spoken with such emotion.

"Marry someone who loves you."

"You can't live without love in your life."

"With love in your life, you can do great things."

On dark nights walking home to an empty place, turning his collar up against the cold, his thoughts would shake him. He would tell himself he should have let Arlene's love come into his life when he had the chance.

I had the chance for something....I really did.

But Rico couldn't go back to that moment in time when Arlene played B-17 and the Flamingos sang a love song and Arlene took him in her arms and held him so close in shadows and candlelight and they slow danced cheek-to-cheek and she gave him the chance for something in his life in a closed private club on a long ago summer night in the year of 1985.

Fast Lane Friends

I'm going to tell you something right from the get-go, and I'm not going to exhibit any restraints to describe it - screw that, I had a bad fucking week. I'm really tensed up. Now I'm not in any way going to apologize for using the F-word in the very first sentence. I don't want to hear, "Oh damn, very first sentence curse word, curse word. Where does he go from here?" Just don't confront me with that. It's just a descriptive adjective that's all it is. Nothing more. It just gives impact and describes the week in a clearer perspective. If someone says they had a bad week, without using the descriptive adjective—so what, who gives a damn. Who wants to hear it?

So this is what I had to deal with at work and I never had a week like this before. It was the week from hell and you've probably had one yourself and be honest, you probably came out with a descriptive adjective or two yourself to describe it. Computers were down, no help desk support available. Can't make any deliveries because union drivers went out on strike. Customers calling with threats, "No deliveries - No checks!" Payroll says our direct deposits didn't go through. Two people quit and they told us no new hires and everybody else will have to take up the slack. Some jerk off from the main office sends a directive stating the company needs a better bottom line or concessions on our benefits will be needed. And on our office bulletin board the office manager posts a notice saying she would like to see a more happy and cheerful and let's all work together aura in the work place. Bullshit. Total bullshit!

Then I cut out of work a little early to get away from all this nonsense and I felt I was going to explode and the car battery conked out on an upper floor of a bi-level parking garage and I am going to have a hell of a time getting the car out of there because tow trucks don't fit in bi-level parking garages.

Just screw all this bullshit. I'm reaching a breaking point.

So it's early Saturday afternoon, thank goodness I'm off and I'm just trying to calm down and chill out and relax and clear my mind from all this nonsense so I figure I'll wolf down a cheese steak or two with tomato sauce and fried onions and munch on some chips and scarf down a few bottles of beer from Denmark in greedy swallows and flip through the channels and see what's on my 26-inch flat screen. You do whatever you need to do to relax.

First show I hit, no desire or energy whatsoever on my part to flip through the cable channels, besides I got a little buzz going on from the bottled beer from Denmark, these three nut balls each with a faraway look in their eyes are seated on a leather couch holding bottles of spring water.

One of the nut balls, tears welling up in his eyes, is clutching some tissues and across from them a head shrinker is seated in an olive tinted wrap-around leather chair, note book in hand, asking the nut balls questions about the trials and tribulations they are facing in everyday life. One of the nut balls on the couch is sobbing and the one seated next to him puts his arm around him trying to console him. Just what I need to give my aura an uplift, a show about depressed whacked out people in need of counseling. How cheerful will this be?

And the head shrinker with his narrow reading glasses perched inches above his forehead, notebook and expensive pen at the ready position, in a clear calming voice says, "Stanley, what you're facing is not that serious. For god sakes grab hold of yourself! Use the tissues and stop the damn sobbing because you're causing a scene and upsetting everyone. You have to have a sense of decorum about yourself for god sakes. If you're not calm, no one around you will be calm. Can you grasp that, damn it?"

Stanley throws some sobs out there followed by a few more.

Then for dramatic effect with his voice elevated sensing the television camera is eyeballing him and just maybe the producers will extend the show for a few more episodes, "Damn it Stanley! Man the hell up! Man the fuck up! Get a grip! Don't you want to walk in the sunshine with a sense of pride and your head held high at some point in your life?"

Now I didn't catch the name of the show on the cable channel when I clicked it on but if I had to render a random guess I think it would be called, "Nut Balls on a Leather Couch Crying Out For Help With a Head Shrinker There to Assist in the Recovery."

So then the consoling nut ball clutching tissues stands up and starts sobbing and gesturing and screaming at the head shrinker, "Don't talk to him that way, how dare you! Because you don't know what it's like to have these emotional scars from childhood and everybody laughs at you and points their fingers at you and tells you the funny farm would be a good place for you because everybody in your family is fucking nuts. That's right....fucking nuts! Everybody in your family.... Everyone! And take them to the nut house too."

I have to admit I was getting caught up in the sob fest. I mean their pain was getting to me, and I was offering mental encouragement for speedy recoveries because the thought of what mental anguish can do to someone, you know going to the funny farm aspect of it, was also starting to get to me.

Now I know I am perfectly normal, at least I think I am, but you never know what a buildup of stress can do to you including being sidetracked from the straight and narrow path you try to walk and winding up sobbing on a leather couch on the nut ball show on cable television.

And then just like that, and I didn't know what was going on, I was shocked, but the guy on the cable show offering consolation was growing weary of shouting at the head shrinker. So all of a sudden it's like a shift of focus is going on and he's trying to get my attention and to talk to me at the same time trying to push his face through the television screen trying to get closer to me for emphasis. I'm thinking, *damn!....How much of this shit did I drink? Am I hallucinating?*

Now he's yelling at me trying to make eye contact. "I'm not nuts. See me trying to console Stanley? Screwballs can't console anyone. Sure I'm unbalanced once in a while. Who isn't? But I'm not going to any nut house as long as I'm thinking clear. I dare them to try to take me to the nut farm! Just let them try and I'll go off!"

I recoiled from the T.V. screen. He continued shouting his face almost on my side of the screen. "Don't believe anything they try to tell you about me. I'm almost normal when I take my meds. I'm innocent of anything they say about me and I can prove it."

Now I'm screaming at the T.V. telling him to stop trying to break into my house thinking my screen's going to get ripped open and that would be a real bitch because I let my Extended Warrantee Service T.V. Contract expire because I was short on cash when the bill came due. To be honest, I missed paying some other bills also.

I was thinking about calling the police but how the hell could I explain what I'm seeing? Then

I'm thinking the cops would probably drag me out of my house handcuffed and all and news clips for the evening's news would announce, "Screwball dragged from his row house in handcuffs. Says someone tried to break into his house through his television screen. Film at eleven." *What would my family and friends think of me then? They'd think I was mentally unstable.*

Somehow I found the remote after a frantic search and I clicked him off, thank god; after the week I had I didn't need any of this nonsense. And as crazy as it sounds it's like I could still hear him yelling at me after the screen went black. I said to myself, *You gotta get the hell out of here for a while. Your head's really screwed up. Go now! Get the hell out now and breathe in some fresh air and suck in some benefits from the sunshine, some vitamin D to build up your bones and improve your mental health and whatever else you get from the sunshine and fresh air. Get the hell out of the house right now before your mental stability gets impaired.*

I know I need it after a week in that airless, windowless, shoe box size cubicle I work in. I feel like I'm working in a closet. And they got these overhead security cameras eyeballing you all the time and just try to check your E-Mail or try to buy a pair of shoes at a discount price online.

Get this, the security cameras actually time you if you have to take a leak so you better be quick about it or they might write you up for stealing company time. I'm reaching a breaking point at that place, I really am, but I realize I have to remain calm after what I just saw on cable television because I don't want to wind up on the nut ball show. I really need the job. I need the salary they toss at us just to keep the wolf from coming through my door and ripping me to shreds and then I will be on collection agency's call lists.

Before I head out I'm thinking *I better freshen up because you never know who you're going to run into outside and you should always want to make a good impression.* So I go to my upstairs bathroom, splash warm sink water on my face, then again, and I look in the mirror. *Damn guy! Look at you! That job has you stressed out to the max. Dark circles under your eyes, you look like a damn raccoon. You gotta make some changes man. Maybe you should make an appointment with the T.V. head shrinker.*

So I head out of my row house (I felt a little wobbly. I gotta stop drinking that beer) and I walk five blocks down the avenue once lined with shade trees and they gave the avenue a nice look against some rundown houses, turn left at a narrow side street, right at another side street, then left at Cheltenham Avenue with the yellow painted mini-market on the corner on my way to the neighborhood park.

Painted in black glossy letters above the mini-market's door an indication of ownership: *Julio's Friendly Neighborhood Mini-Market*. And underneath that the store's hours: "We Never Close and We Speak Spanish." So much black and yellow the place looks like a beehive and I can visualize a sales clerk inside wearing black slacks and a yellow shirt and above his shirt pocket his name in black letters, "Julio Ramos."

All I want to do is sit on a park bench for a while, breathe in fresh air I never breathed in before, and block out any thoughts about going back to work on Monday because that place just sucks out every ounce of energy you have stored up inside you.

And just then, damn it! I get intercepted. Coming out of the yellow painted neighborhood mini-market with black drop-down iron security gates, walking towards me eyeballing me at the same time wearing a soiled yellow tank-top undershirt and carrying two extra-large size bags of cat litter, is the neighborhood nut ball, Freddy, "The Dynamite Man," Pachadda. All I wanted to do is get to that park for a while and relax on a park bench and clear my head and I almost got this panic attack because I just went through this at home with the nut ball trying to get at me through my flat screen and here's another one coming right at me live and in person.

Now Freddy drops the extra-large size bags of cat litter, he lights a cigarette and he starts gesturing wildly at who knows what and I am searching for an escape route so I can get the hell away from him. To be honest, I have no idea who spread the rumor that Freddy was a nut ball. It certainly wasn't me. I would never entertain the thought of spreading rumors with the intent of slandering someone's character, especially on the side of being a nut ball. I might say he's a little whacked out but that's as far as I would go.

I do believe this however. Newspapers don't lie. A few weeks ago the headlines and story were out there in bold print. "Construction worker, Frederick Pachadda, 57, uses too much dynamite. Ruins newly-constructed highway. Some workers injured. Medical tests show Mr. Pachadda has signs of reduced mental capacity due to suffering on the job concussions. His miscalculation of dynamite used in previous demolition jobs the probable cause of his mental impairment."

Then this for which he was criminally charged: "Disgraced construction worker charged with severely damaging genitals of neighborhood thug remotely setting off dynamite placed under seat of his newly purchased ten speed bicycle. Trial date is scheduled for July 22nd in City Hall Courtroom number 337. Defendant claims innocence."

Now Freddy looked the part of being a dynamite man in the hot weather when he walked around in his soiled tank-top undershirt. Years ago after he dropped out of medical school—can you believe that?—Freddy got deluxe tattoos in a rundown tattoo parlor across the Delaware River in Camden N.J. On his upper right arm he had this red dynamite plunger with wires attached and wrapped around his arm leading to sticks of dynamite stuck in the opening of a gold mine or something like that.

On the other arm there's a hand having pressed the yellow plunger handle down and what was left of the gold mine which was blown to pieces. His lower arm looked like a jig-saw puzzle and if you looked real close there could have been blown up pieces of a gold miner caught in the explosion. His arms looked like a scene from a wild-wild west movie that you could see at your nearby multiplex, and if you saw it in 3-D it would probably cost you at least twenty bucks. That's what Freddy did with his first paycheck in the dynamite business—getting deluxe high end tattoos in Camden, N.J.

Before he took the dynamite job, Freddy had aspirations of being a disaster doctor who sets and repairs broken bones and limbs and things like that after a catastrophe happens. But after being in medical school for a while and thumbing through his medical text books, he got squeamish thinking he wouldn't have the guts to saw away a broken piece of bone or whatever else you had to do to repair someone who got all busted up.

Now Freddy's supervisors saw signs of a dynamite man in a slightly downward spiral. One said, "You try to make eye contact with Freddy and it's like lights are on but nobody's home." But the overall consensus from the supervisor's team was sure his brain must be a little bit rattled after all the explosions he set off but other than that he seems okay.

There was a final small job coming up that had to be done to meet a ten-day deadline so they gave Freddy detailed instructions as to the precise amount of dynamite needed to complete the job. Three times they went over it with him. The instructions were both written and oral just to make sure.

There was this hundred-foot-high rock formation and they needed just a little space to provide a shoulder for a newly constructed highway. Just blow up a couple of rocks, that's all he had to do. This rock formation was stone cold ugly and it looked like it was made up of millions of pieces of black coal that somehow got glued together when the whole universe was formed. Even with the deadline they were facing, a roadblock came up. This nearby preservation group said you just can't blow up rocks that are millions and billions of years old and date back to the creation of earth and they threatened to take the construction company to court and sue them for millions and millions of dollars.

A supervisor came up with an idea. He said his son is in college studying rocks and rock formations and he would have him come out and take a look at the rocks and send the preservation group a letter stating the formation is nowhere near a billion years old and as such the formation has no relevance whatsoever.

The letter went like this:

Dear Honored and Respected Preservation Group Members,

Please be advised I have inspected the rock formation and found their true age to be in the 35,000 year range. I used complex chemical testing and laser beams to help me come up with this figure. The rocks do not date to the earth's early formation around the time the big bang theory took place.

Respectfully yours,

C. S. Eshington, Rock Specialist.

The letter worked. They never heard from the preservation group again and the project went on. Everybody on the construction team was elated because they would meet the deadline and hefty cash bonuses would be paid for all workers to share in. Spirits were certainly high. Cement truck driver, Bobby Ciparella, may have jumped the gun on the hefty cash bonuses; still he told his wife to go ahead to have the twins, Kristen and Kayla, fitted for dental braces, get ten-year-old Kenny contact lenses and spare no expense.

Then the unthinkable happened while everyone was figuring out the amount of the hefty cash bonuses they would receive and what they could blow the bonus cash on. The damn unthinkable. Freddy misunderstood or misread the detailed instructions he was given and with his rattled brain he used ten times the amount needed for the job's requirement. The instructions stipulated five pounds of dynamite; somehow Freddy added a zero and used fifty pounds.

Freddy blew up the whole damn rock formation. The whole damn formation. Fifteen feet of busted rocks covered the newly constructed four-lane highway for 125 feet busting up asphalt and all the construction equipment was smashed to pieces. There were worker injuries, none serious, and those not injured wanted to beat the piss out of Freddy, especially Bobby Ciparella because he had to face his wife and tell her no dental braces or contact lenses.

In the middle of all the chaos after the explosion, Freddy's staggering around aimlessly over some rocks looking toward the heavens seemingly pleading for answers from above, a dazed look on his face and he is shouting, "What the hell could've happened here?" The preservation group later filed a law suit against everyone who worked for the construction company from cement truck drivers to upper echelon C.E.O's. They wanted millions of dollars.

The construction company was forced out of business because no one would hire them to move even a pile of sand.

The supervisor's son, C. S. Eshington, Rock Specialist, was jailed for using phony credentials.

After they pulled Freddy down from the rock pile, he resisted all the way, they fired him right on the spot and he was still yelling, "What the hell happened here? I've been framed!"

Bobby Ciparella was on his cell-phone telling his wife to put a stop on the dental braces and contact lenses and then he tried to get at Freddy to beat the piss out of him.

So there I was in the sunshine and the heat and humidity on Cheltenham Avenue and it hit me that today is the longest day of the year and I'm thinking I should be doing something special today. I mean you gotta do something special on the longest day of the year. And I have to admit I was feeling a little bit hammered from the beer I drank and being hammered is no way to celebrate the longest day of the year.

I was trapped. I felt the bars of the drop-down security gates pressed against my back and I was cursing the damn mini-market for not rolling them up when they're opened for business. Freddy was right in my face and on either side of him was a giant sized bag of cat litter blocking my path of escape. He's talking fast, about 60 M.P.H. if you would want to equate it to automobile travel.

He said, "I didn't blow them damn rocks up and I didn't blow that kid's nuts off!"

I said: "Ah huh! Ah huh! Ah huh! Did you get lawyered up?" Hell, everybody in the neighborhood knew about the kid's nuts. Guys hanging out on corners outside steak and hoagie shops talked about it.

Seventeen year old Sal Di'Puchio, A.K.A. *Scarface Sal*, said, "I'm glad it wasn't my nuts that got blown off. I want to be able to keep my family lineage going on. My kids will have something to offer generations to come."

Besides the newspaper headlines, they saw the film clip for Your News at Eleven Tonight:

"Highway screw-up dynamite man goes to trial for damaging teen's genitals. Pleads innocence. Claims he was set up. Faces jail time."

I was trapped, but what could I do? Somehow, and I don't know where this feeling was coming from, I had this heroic aura sweeping over me feeling if I didn't hear Freddy out he might have some spare dynamite around and he might blow up the neighborhood. I'm reasoning, *By listening to Freddy, I'm obtaining salvation from that. I hope the neighborhood appreciates what I'm doing here, listening to Freddy.*

I felt like yelling out: "Hey! People out there. Pay attention! Can you see what I'm trying to do here? I'm trying to save your houses."

Freddy's telling me he was framed and he was the victim of medical malpractice and evaluation in the workplace. "They knew I was seeing double and having these headaches and I couldn't think straight and I had a concussion or two or three or four but they said, 'Don't worry, you'll get over it."

With all this yellow and black around me and it looks like a beehive maybe a swarm of bees will fly out the front door of the mini-market and they'll start munching on Freddy and scare him off.

So with salvation thoughts running through my head, and I don't want any bees swarming around because they would probably start chomping on me and I wouldn't want that because I don't look good in lumps, I look over Freddy's shoulder and I see a ray of hope.

Slowly pulling up at the curb as if it is on a secret mission, a fifteen year old rusted burgundy S.U.V. with Bobby Ciparella at the wheel along with four of his construction worker friends. Bobby's steering and shouting, "You son -of-a-bitch Freddy! Because of you, no dental braces for Kristen and Kayla! I'm gonna beat the piss out of you ....You son-of-a-bitch! And no contact lenses either!"

Freddy yelled back neck veins pulsating. "Get the hell out of my neighborhood you idiot. And I don't care about your twins and their crooked teeth."

They all got out of the S.U.V. so fast. I thought one came out through the sun roof, and somehow I noticed they're all wearing tan hi-top heavy duty construction work boots with thick lug soles and steel toes and the heel of the boots must weigh fifteen pounds each and you could probably pull a boat with the shoe laces and if some Zombies invaded the neighborhood from the cemetery up the street these construction workers turned goons could stomp the hell out of them and end the invasion and save the neighborhood and they would all be viewed as heroes and appear on cable television news broadcasts and an overly-coiffured news anchor flaunting excessive facial make-up would ask in a stoic tone, "Now please tell our audience exactly how you stopped the Zombie invasion from the cemetery."

Hearing the commotion inside the mini-market while paying for the three cartons of cigarettes she purchased for herself and other coughing family members, Arlene D'Pietro, put $100.00 on the counter and then quickly stepped outside to try and figure out what was going on.

Not even thinking about Zombies, only about saving his life, Freddy bolts through the front door of the mini-market, he knocks down giant sized bags of cat litter in the aisle of the rear stockroom as a roadblock, out the back door he goes down the driveway and around the block into his row house through the basement door and he hides under the steps leading to his kitchen.

Now under his basement steps, Freddy's searching the heavens seeking answers as to where the extra zero on the job slip came from but nothing came to him probably because from under his steps he couldn't even see the heavens.

Breaking his concentration, five overweight cats as a team start meowing at his feet begging for food and Freddy tells them he's trying to figure something out and to stop the damn meowing. Before he bolted, Freddy asked me to watch his cat litter for him. Bobby Ciparella gets in my face surrounded by his construction-worker friends and I think one of them was wearing brass knuckles, "If you know what's good for you, tell us where he lives! Ya know we all lost our jobs. And benefits too."

You could tell by hearing him talk that Bobby enjoyed being a bully with his construction friends there to back him up. He said to himself, *I like this. This is the new me. Mr. Tough Guy.*

I spoke back, talking like I had a pack of goons behind me, "I don't know who the hell he is! Find out for yourself!"

Bobby says, "Lemme introduce ya to some of my friends from the fast lane. I call them my fast lane friends and they got brass knuckles and brass balls. Show him, Jerome!...your knuckles not your..."

Jerome thrusts his hand high aloft above his

head sun glistening off his knuckles. "Anyone screws anyone of us we get even real fast. Got that? "

I noticed Bobby punching his fist into his open hand probably as a threatening gesture and I wondered if his I.Q. level was any higher than 78. "He stopped me and asked me to help him with his giant-sized bags of cat litter. There's the cat litter right there."

"I'm on my way to the park to relax on a park bench after a hard week at work. Wanna hear about it?" I'm wearing my sunglasses and they were doing me good because I could look out at this moron and he couldn't look in and see what I was thinking. Acting like I had some goons backing me up, I told him to get out of my face.

Bobby Ciparella wanted nothing to do with me. He just wanted to find Freddy and beat the hell out of him over the loss of the bonus money and his job because his teenaged twins were tormenting him telling him thanks to him no boys will ask them out on dates because of their crooked teeth and they will have emotional scars for the rest of their lives and they'll probably never get married.

And if there wasn't enough tension in the air, Bobby's telling his goons to spread out over the neighborhood and knock on doors and find Freddy so they start scurrying down the driveways and side streets, Julio comes running out of his mini-market shouting in Spanish about Freddy fucking up his back room knocking cat litter bags all around. Bobby bolts through the mini-market trying to catch up with Freddy. *Spare me this*, I'm saying this to myself, *I just need some peace and quiet*.

Besides being pissed off, Bobby and his friends were really agitated. Before leaving out to find Freddy and beat the hell out of him, they stopped off at a rival construction company and applied for jobs as a group. They were given some cold hard facts. "No one will hire anyone one of you. You're all blackballed from here to Utah! You're all guilty by association. No, make that guilty of association to stupidity. You'll never get jobs after working for a company that ruined 125 feet of a newly constructed highway. Sounds like your dynamite man had a few loose screws in his head. Weren't those rocks he blew up a billion years old or something like that?"

Courtroom 337 City Hall was jam packed with spectators waiting for the start of the "Dynamite Man trial." Freddy's lawyer was seated at the defense table shuffling through legal documents hoping his client listened to the pre-trial advice he gave him.

There was quite a bit of chit-chat going on in the courtroom.

"His neighbors are edgy. They think he'll blow up some houses."

"Hope they search him for dynamite. Are we safe in here?"

"He could blow up the courtroom by remote control."

"I don't wanna see pictures of the kid's damaged nuts."

"I heard his co-workers tried to string him up."

"Someone said they found dynamite buried at the judge's house."

Check list in hand, Freddy's lawyer was going over it. Number one on the list: Wear a conservative suit so you make a good impression on the judge and jury, and he wondered where his client was. He looked over his shoulder, saw Freddy coming down the center aisle, and he almost threw his stacks of legal documents in the air he was so pissed off.

He wanted to just get up and go but he couldn't because he needed the fee he would receive for defending Freddy because his wife is suing him for divorce and she's got a ball-busting lawyer. Freddy's walking down the aisle and he looks like a stick of dynamite. He's wearing reddish tinted trousers, a yellow shirt and a very narrow black knit tie.

"What in god's name did I tell you about making a good impression to impress everyone that you're a normal guy and a suit could do that. You look like a stick of dynamite! Where the hell's the damn suit? A navy suit! Any kind of suit! Where are your brains coming in looking like that! The jury's going to think if you look like dynamite you gotta be guilty."

The lawyer had to let it go at that. He saw the distant faraway look in Freddy's eyes and besides he had to discuss with Freddy that he faced future charges after the trial under the Leopold Loss of Lineage Lamentation Law and Statute. Now this statute goes back a ways. Billy Leopold was high school drop-out who forged his educational background and he got a job with the city taking out trolley car tracks that once crisscrossed the city. The tool of his trade was a newly-invented pneumatic powered jack hammer that could bust up a cubic foot of concrete in two minutes. The trouble was the pneumatic power jack hammer gave off tremendous vibrations and after working nine hours a day for six months the vibrations traveled up Billy's legs and they damaged his sperm producing organ. When Billy found out he couldn't father children he broke down and sobbed but he took solace in the thought that he was going to sue the city and the company that mass produced the power jack hammer. Billy received a substantial damage award and he thanked the trial judge and jury saying, "It rips my heart out that my lineage stops here. But a shiny new red convertible should put ointment on my wounds. Your honor, thank you for the ointment."

Freddy's lawyer told him, "If this kid can't reproduce when he gets older, you'll have to compensate him for the pain and suffering of not being able to pass on his family lineage." Freddy responded, "The world will be a better place if he can't have any fucked up kids."

After placing his right hand on the bible and swearing to tell the whole truth, Freddy gave animated testimony as to what happened on the day in question. Freddy's lawyer told him what to say and not to say but Freddy went on from there and his lawyer couldn't stop the oncoming train wreck. Pointing to his head and swirling his finger he said, "Sure I've had a concussion or two or three and my marbles are a little loose from setting off dynamite and once in a while I get fogged out a little bit and my brain is a little rattled but I remember what happened with that kid clear as day."

He said after being fired from his job he hunkered down in his row house afraid to go out because neighbors were protesting outside his house hoisting signs in the air. One sign exclaimed in large red letters: MOVE THE HELL OUT!!! YOUR'RE NOT GOING TO BLOW UP THE NEIGHBORHOOD!!!

So Freddy's isolated in his row house, he's getting depressed, his meds aren't kicking in, and he gets up early one morning and heads out to a high-end bicycle shop on Frankford Avenue. Freddy test rides and buys a 30 speed deluxe all-terrain silver and black bicycle and he tells the salesman he wants to ride it on city streets and in the deep woods. He also buys needed accessories: A matching silver and black helmet with a rear view mirror attached to it. Bicycle gloves and protective knee pads, bicycling shoes and matching apparel and wrap around white framed sun glasses.

The salesman wanting extra commissions

suggested a heavy-duty bicycle lock but he was shrugged off, Freddy saying, "Don't worry. I got the security part covered and down pat. Don't you worry about that."

Freddy slapped $956.00 all in crisp fresh new bills of higher denomination, some of it probably from his last paycheck as a dynamite man, and before the bills hit the counter the salesman already figured out his take on the sale and he deducted that amount from his rent which was a month behind. So after getting every dollar he could from Freddy, now he just wants him out the door and gone so he can wait on the next customer and make more commissions. Trying to show the customer service one deserves, the salesman opens the door and he gestures toward the avenue for Freddy and his new all-terrain bike and he shouts as Freddy rides off.

"Ride off into the sunshine!"

"May you have blue skies and green lights!"

"May your gears always mesh and your tires spin forward!"

"Farewell! Farewell! to you and come back to buy more stuff!"

The bicycle store manager tells his salesman, "Great sale; now get the next customer."

The salesman responds, "Out the door went an accident just waiting to happen. He'll probably get hit by a bus and wind up in the E.R."

So Freddy rides out over Frankford Avenue heading south with the sun in his face and the wind rushing through his helmet and he's thinking someone should be there to write a song about him and a good name for it would be, "Air Rushing Through My Helmet On A Sunny Day."

He's riding under the elevated train structure past Bridge Street and he turns down a narrow side street to install his security system on his newly purchased 30-speed all-terrain bicycle. He securely tapes under the seat a small packet of dynamite which he could set off with a remote control device he just somehow happened to bring home from his demolition job.

He goes back on Frankford Avenue and he stops to admire the ornate façade at the same level of the elevated train structure of the long ago closed Circle movie theater. *I think I'll visit the old neighborhood wherever that might be,* he's thinking to himself reminiscing about the Saturday double features plus cartoons he saw at the Circle Theater years ago. Orthodox Street is straight ahead and he figures he'll head over it and see what he runs into. Riding through a rundown neighborhood past Darrah Street, he's feeling confident should anyone try fucking with either him or his new bike because he'll blow them to pieces. Crossing Torresdale Avenue and through the curve in Orthodox Street then under the railroad bridge straight ahead at the corner of Tacony Street across the street from the long ago closed *Ritz Neighborhood Laundromat*, he sees *Mario's Star Direct to You Pizza Place.*

His thought process is twisted up and he's a little out of kilter and he thinks years ago he went into Mario's, ordered a pizza and ate it and he split the scene without paying for it. Freddy's mind is playing tricks on him now and mentally he's on a downward spiral. *Maybe instead of concussions the dynamite gave me brain cancer and I'll be dead in a few days. I could have a brain artery bust on me and I'll be dead on the spot and I hope it doesn't happen in the street because a bus could run over me and I won't look too good in a coffin.*

Now he's feeling remorse and restitution is needed so he goes inside to settle accounts. Right now he's feeling pretty good about himself walking into Mario's about to do the restitution thing. *There's a lotta good in me, I abound in integrity. Yes I do!* he's telling himself. Mario's at the pizza ovens, tourist attractions of Italy tattooed on his arms, twirling pizza dough high aloft and he's wearing a greasy apron and he has a greasy hand towel draped over his shoulder. Business is bad in the rundown neighborhood and Freddy tells Mario his story about a possible long ago debt and Mario's mood is suddenly uplifted thinking cash is coming in with no pizzas going out.

Freddy hands Mario thirty bucks for the imagined unpaid-for pizza plus tip and interest. Mario's overwhelmed with joy. Such honesty he has never seen in this neighborhood. A real joy fest was going on brought on by the joining of restitution and sheer honesty. They almost embraced.

Then Mario tosses the greasy hand towel aside and he starts singing in broken English and old country accent: "Kay-Lida Mangiare Someone Ellsa's Pizza Pie. May Essi Die Sans Lingua." Translation: If someone eats pizza from another place, may he die without a tongue. Mario sings two verses, his hands on the pizza cutting table, acting as if he is performing at some grand opera theater somewhere in southern Italy. He adds, "Truly, my faith in mankind has been fully restored."

Breaking this aria up, a voice loud and clear and chaos from outside. "Look what I found. No one's here. Its mine! I'm taking it!"

Freddy rushes outside and he sees the heist going down. By this time the kid's halfway down the block, Freddy's screaming, "Get the fuck back here, I just spent nine hundred dollars for everything," and over his right shoulder, without even looking back, the kid extends his middle finger towards Freddy. That was a mistake.

Freddy pulls out his remote control dynamite setting-off device and without an ounce of guilt he presses the red button and this... BAM! sound echoes up and down the street and people are running out of their houses to see what's going on.

Freddy's newly purchased silver and black bicycle along with the kid who ripped it off, rocket twenty feet in the air, trailing behind it a plume of acrid smoke. On his downward trip the kid lands in the bed of an abandoned, rusted pickup truck and he's screaming, "He blew my nuts off. I won't be able to have kids. How can I continue my lineage?"

Right now Freddy's honesty and integrity aura is gone and escape and self-preservation kicks in. Freddy flips the remote control device in the bin of a passing trash truck but some of the kid's friends see it and they start yelling as a police car pulls up. "He did it, and he tossed the remote control dynamite setting-off device with the red button in the trash truck. He blew Chico's nuts off!"

Chico turned out to be okay. Just some powder burns around his nuts. But tests will have to be conducted to see if he could extend his family lineage.

The judge asked Freddy if he had anything to say to the court. Freddy stood up from the defense table; his lawyer tried to yank him down. He hiked up his pants and adjusted his tie and he said, "I want to go back to medical school and take tests and be a doctor. I think I can help people who get hurt in dynamite explosions anywhere in the world. And I don't know nothing about Chico and his nuts." The judge ordered Freddy to be held for psychological testing before passing sentence.

So I finally made it to the park. What a relief. Just what I needed—a park bench and some fresh air to restore my well-being. I have to admit I was feeling a lot better and I didn't feel hammered anymore and the tense feeling I had was drifting away. I was looking at the trees getting all blissed out breathing fresh air and somehow a few thoughts hit me. I don't know where they came from but they were there. Some things just seemed a lot clearer to me now.

I can't go back to that job on Monday.

There has to be something better out there somewhere.

I'm tired of that place day after day sucking all of that energy out of me.

Every day I leave that place I feel emotionally drained.

I have to get out of this neighborhood real quick. There's too many screwballs moving in and before you know it there will be a head shrinker's office on every corner.

And I have to get somebody back in my life and hold on to her. Not like the last time. That's for damn sure. I can't screw up again. You just need someone to hold on to when things are falling apart and in the middle of the cold black nights they take pieces out of you and you need to reach out to her and ask. "Please…hold on to me and help me get through the night."

It's a screwed-up world out there and you need a little human touch factor in your life. And you tell yourself, *Everyone else seems to have it, I can see it, why not me?…I need it…how do I get it? Damn, I really need it!*

And if you should have this person in your

life to hold on to in the middle of the cold black nights when things are falling apart and they take pieces out of you, whatever you do, don't ever risk losing it. Don't let that happen.

Because if you do, what will you do?

What the hell will you do!?

I. D. G. A. F.

THE HISTORICAL AND PSYCHOLOGICAL RESEARCH

"EYE-DEE-GAFF!"

"EYE-DEE-GAFF!"

"I WON'T FUCKIN' GO!"

"NO! I WON'T FUCKIN' GO! "

(Rebellious war chant said to have its' origin during the Great War of 966 A.D., give or take a few decades.) (Further, according to historical documents, "EYE-DEE-GAFF" is the correct way to pronounce I.D.G.A F.)

Face fucking furious facts.

Everything is so tense today.

You're always on edge.

The pressure never lets up.

You haven't had a calm relaxing moment in months.

And it's 95 blast furnace degrees outside and everything is hot to the touch, and you can't even think straight with the blasted heat and deal with all the bullshit going on in your life. All you need is for one more person to play with you, just one more, and you're going to explode.

It's like you're always walking a thin line, dealing with this, dealing with that, and one miscalculated step and you take the plunge down a dark elevator shaft and it's the sudden stop at the bottom that gets you securely strapped to a canvas stretcher and slammed into the back of a emergency rescue vehicle then high speeding, red lights flashing, sirens wailing, towards your local E. R., and you're somewhere between unconscious but not quite half-dead. All you want to do is let out a couple of ear piercing moans to let the medical staff know that you're coming out of it, and please, "Don't send me to a mental facility."

But this E.R. doctor has your eyelids clamped open, medical flashlight beaming in, and through the swirling fog you can almost make out his prognosis: "This is the worst case of stupidity I have ever seen in my twenty years at P.G.H. Besides this idiot, it's been twenty years of stitching other morons up after their drunken weekend brawls then trying to coax them to go out and have a good and productive life knowing full damn well that I will probably see them again next weekend. And how in creation do you take a swan dive down a five story elevator shaft?"

"Fucking-A," added the head nurse, at the

end of her fourteen hour shift.

Your local head doctors in their oak-paneled offices complete with full body sized leather couches are having a field day stuffing their financial portfolios with aggressive stock funds. They summer in the islands under azure skies sucking in cool refreshing breezes while sipping on exotic drinks with miniature umbrellas sticking out from the top of the glass. All this relaxation from insurance checks they get from dealing with your never ending misery.

And you think they really want to help straighten you out.

"Come on in and lie down and tell me all of your troubles. Don't hold anything back. Here, grab some tissues and a bottle of spring water. Don't worry. Relax. We can sedate you if you like."

"It seems like nobody can help me....And I don't know where to turn....I feel so lost all of the time." You stammer like an idiot.

"Now, come on. Come on now. We'll get to the bottom of all this nonsense and sort things out. Yes we will. And then once again you will be a productive member of society and you can walk in the sunshine again with your head held high."
Yeah!

You're joking…Right!

Get real!

You take three steps out of his office after he shuts the door and he moans to himself after first making sure that your insurance policy is up to date. "Boo-Fucking-Hoo."

A slight pause, then. "Another sorry lifelong loser I have to deal with and listen to their never ending whining until they're ready for the nut house."

Believe this; it's a fact: If you're this whacked out that you have to lie down on a leather couch in an oak-paneled office and dab at your eyes with the head doctor's cheap tissues while you pour out your troubled heart and soul between gulps of bottled spring water. Then you're going to be whacked out for a long, long time.

Do not expect any immediate positive results or life altering changes.

These are tense times, and there is always something out there just waiting to screw you up. But still, you just have to grab hold of yourself. Realize this: You are a decent person, unless you are an out-and-out jerk off. Your back's just screwed to the wall and this giant fist has you by the throat choking the living hell out of you. Be strong. Get a grip on yourself. Just because you're all twisted up on the inside and you can't even function day to day, doesn't mean you can't put on an air of normalcy on the outside.

It's called: "Conditioning of the self."

Try it...... "Conditioning of the self."

Then everyone will say: "Hey! Look at that nice normal guy with a smile on his face walking down the street projecting an image of self-confidence and decorum. Everybody should be like him and the world will be a better place for everyone."

So try to work on this basic premise. You're all twisted up on the inside and you can't even function day to day; yet you project a normal appearance on the outside so everybody thinks you're okay. This is self-conditioning at work.

Whatever you do!

Whatever you do!

Do not lose it on a dark night and go looking for a high bridge over deep water. Do not peer down at the murky water from the high up railing blabbing out your sorry life story and all at once blurt out: EYE-DEE-GAFF! Then again: EYE-DEE-GAFF!

Which means: "I DON'T GIVE A FUCK."

(Which somehow has its' origin from the proper sequence of the letters: I. D. G. A. F.) Forget the sequence of the letters for a minute. Don't try to figure out who put this stuff together. You're ready to mentally snap, and you just might jump.

And it's so easy to get this way today when your whole world is screwed up big time and you feel you have no other recourse but to scream out "EYE-DEE-GAFF!" at the top of your lungs.

Just let it go!

Let it out!

SCREAM IT THE FUCK OUT!

You will feel better.

Trust me; you will.

You will feel this sudden rush and it will feel as if you can breathe again.

The reasons you feel this way are everywhere. You're not immune from them. Nobody is. Don't think for a minute that you're the only one that's messed up out there.

A few examples:

Your management team comes to talk to you at your work station at the chemical plant and they're wearing this sinister look on their faces. Right away, this is bad karma. Their put on soothing voice tells you you're screwed before they get a chance to blurt anything out.

"You've probably heard the rumors going around lately and we just want to clarify...."

"Whadda you mean....rumors? I don't pay attention to...."

"Sure you do, everybody does, it's only natural; we're all human here."

"I don't. I just try and do my...."

"Just listen, please; this hurts everybody, but if you give it a shot.... it's for the overall good of everyone. We're all in this together don't you know?"

As if offering a reassuring (everything is going to be okay and you won't get laid off) human touch, the supervisory tall blonde in the expensive navy business suit reaches out and touches your arm.

"Hey! We're a team here! You know that. We're like family here." The blonde pontificates, soothing voice and all, giving your arm a little rub, slightly nodding her head in the glow given off by her other management team members.

"I'm not in the mood. Please don't play with me. I'm behind on my rent and they might come for my car late at night. Don't you have any idea what it's like to be at the bottom of the pecking order?"

Just like that, as if she was just bitten by a

snake, the tall blonde harshly retracts her reassuring human touch and turns dead serious.

"Now just listen....."

This won't be good for you.

"We're going to be doing a little down-sizing here for the intent purpose of a better bottom line for the company, and guess who has to carry the ball a lot more? We all do. It's not just a 'you thing.' And please sign here to okay your contribution of a ten-percent reduction in your pay to help the company attain a better bottom line."

Most companies have this as their mission statement: "We are going to suck out every ounce of energy you have in your entire body. Every ounce of your energy will be depleted. And when we are done with you, you will be like a bowl of Jell-O. And we want to accomplish our mission statement at a reduced rate of compensation."

Right off, I know what you're thinking. You want to tell them to get screwed. You really do. It is a perfectly normal human reaction.

Do not harbor any feelings of guilt deep inside yourself over your reaction. Anyone else would feel the same way under the exact situation.

But think about this for a second before you go nuts.

Do you have another job lined up?

Did you go to Harvard?

Is there an ongoing cash flow in your family?

No? Then what other options do you have at your disposal?

They know they got you by the balls.

Better to just suck things up even if it is at a reduced rate of compensation.

At least you can pay some of your bills and try to keep the wolf from your door so that he can't come in and rip your head right off from your shoulders.

Another issue of major importance nearly everyone you speak to is fully aware of. This being the ongoing, you always need it, everyone else seems to have it...why not me?...how do I get it? ...human touch factor.

You're just sick and tired of going home day after day to an empty place so you go out and try to meet someone. At this stage in your life, with all the misery you're dealing with, anyone with half a brain will work. All you want to do is see a movie with someone, or go bowling with them, and then after bowling take them to the new taco place that just opened and they advertise 99-cent specials and they stay open until midnight. Be assured that this feeling of the need to bond with someone is perfectly normal. I mean who wants to go it alone all of the time? The feeling is like a vapor that you suck in through your pores and it becomes a part of your very being. And maybe if you really connect, and it's only human nature, you just want a little human touch in your life. That little human touch factor that can make you feel as if you are not all alone in this messed up world. You scream out in the night for it: "PLEASE! WHOEVER HAS ANYTHING TO DO WITH THIS. PLEASE.... SEND ME SOMEBODY!"

....ANYBODY!"

But basically, it just comes down to this; and again it's a normal human desire—you just want to get laid once in a while. In actuality, it's not just a wham-bam grunting and groaning physical satisfaction thing we're talking about here.

No! No! Not at all!

We're talking true intimacy here. It's that middle of the dark night thing when everything is so screwed up and you just want to reach out to someone and plead:

"Please..."

"Please hold on to me,...and...help me get through the night."

"Please....just take me in your arms and

hold me close."

Should you have this matter of trust reaching out to someone in the middle of the dark night ability, for heaven's sake, don't ever let it slip through your fingers.

Where would you be without it?

Where...?

What will you do when the screwed up dark nights come one after another then another and another and it seems like they take pieces out of you?

So you meet someone who you think is really special and level headed at the neighborhood corner bar where they shoot darts and drink boilermakers and the combined I. Q. of the regulars who congregate there is minus two-hundred and sixty-seven. This is a bad signal right from the get go.

What do you expect to pick up at a corner bar?

Where are your brains?

Didn't the rumors that she could knock off twelve straight shots and still stand up without holding on to the bar trouble you? And she tells you during the eighties she was stoned out of her mind most of the time but during her lucid moments she bought a second hand guitar and tried to write songs about growing up under the Frankford El. Her scattered few lucid moments produced a few lines and she said she couldn't understand why they didn't evolve into a monster selling concept album.

This is as far as she got during the whole decade:

"Zoom! Zoom! Zoom!"

"Here comes the high up rush hour silver streaked elevated train."

"Roar! Roar! Roar!"

"Whiz by the station oh high up elevated train, because the racket is doing nothing but fucking with my brain."

This....This for the whole damn decade.

And you sucked it all in when she told you if this album had actually come out, there were hidden messages in there that could actually make people's lives better.

Just what the hell gives here anyhow?

What the hell gives?

Aren't you the same guy who always runs his mouth off about wanting to connect with a chic and sophisticated uptown girl with high cheek bones and intelligent eyes who should also have attributes of: wit, charm, skill, precision, knowledge, good looks, winning disposition, great personality, an aura of decorum, and being fluent in at least one other language?

Just a question about the attributes you require from this chic and sophisticated uptown girl with high cheek bones and intelligent eyes that you will never meet. What exactly are your skill and knowledge levels?

Anyhow.

Your heart soars.

You shed actual tears of joy.

You feel tingling sensations surging through your body whenever she speaks your name.

And you do all these things, the movies and the bowling and the tacos. And your life is just full of blue skies and green lights, and you're so happy and your insides aren't twisted up anymore, and you can somewhat function again and take on the world so you call your head doctor and tell him to get screwed.

Are you really that stupid?

Are you really?

There are times when you have to learn a valuable lesson about life. And this is certainly one of them. It goes something like this: Don't ever be too quick to pick up the phone and tell your head doctor to get screwed.

Here's why. And really try to grasp this if you can. Although it might be hard with your limited mentality.

After a great night of bowling for dollars, and after munching on 99-cent tacos and the prospects for getting laid look half decent, she starts playing mind games with you while you're licking up taco crumbs from the taco wrapping paper. So for a good verbal connection, some old codger at the corner table is having a serious bout of whooping cough wheezing and choking on his saliva, she leans over the table littered with taco crumbs. And she has this look in her eyes and it doesn't take a rocket scientist to figure out that it's shaft time for you. Just like a moron you lean over the taco crumbs for a better audio reception to overcome the old man's bout of whooping cough all the while hoping she's going to ask you up to her place for a little foreplay and whatever comes next.

Then you get real with yourself and you fully comprehend you're not going to get your rocks off tonight. As a matter of fact, it probably won't happen for a long time.

Suddenly, one thought runs through your

mind.

It hits you like a runaway bus traveling at a high rate of speed.

You hope your head doctor is an understanding and forgiving person and he will answer your call and honor the medical oath he took even though you left the message on his answering machine telling him to get screwed and that you no longer need his services.

Now it hits you that happiness is such a fleeting thing. Here today; and you're fucked up tomorrow.

She tells you still leaning over littered taco crumbs: "I just wanted to tell you that my cell-phone kind of disappeared, and I don't know where it got to, or what happened to it, or who took it or whatever. And I don't like the thought of going out and buying another one, you know these salespeople are such morons and nothing that you need is ever on sale. I mean there could be some serious communication problems between us from here on out."

She then sips some semi-cold sugar free ice tea and she eyeballs you over the soda cup to see how much damage she's already done. She's feeling pretty good right now knowing that she's breaking your stones.

She knows she can really do a job on you.

"What are you trying to tell me?"

"Please, don't play with me."

"Don't do this to me!"

"Please just listen," she continues, lighting a cigarette and giving her head a little shake. "This upsets me too; I have emotions too. I mean I'm only human, like you. Hey! I got feelings. I do."

Your neck veins are pulsating and anything you ever learned about having an aura of decorum about yourself has just split the scene.

"And I never seem to have any change on me, and my phone card got stolen and I don't know how. So don't expect any calls from me for a while. I have an idea though: Maybe you can drop me a note at my place and I'll get back to you."

You wanted to rip her face off.

"Drop you a note!"

You're so pissed off you can't even see straight.

"You'll get back to me!"

And you were going to take her home to meet your family.

"You evil bitch you!"

Then you really loose it.

Try to grab hold of yourself. Remember:

Self-conditioning at work.

Please try!

Please try hard!

"Are you crazy!? ...ARE YOU CRAZY!? What are you trying to do to me? Send me to the nut farm? I've been taking you bowling! Look where I bring you! This place just opened! I just called my shrink the other day and told him to get screwed!"

Calm down!

Calm the hell down!

The other people in here are trying to enjoy the cuisine and engage in a little relaxing chit-chat after a hard week working for minimum wages in run down factories where they make cardboard boxes, sprinkler heads or toaster ovens.

And here you are; screwing up their night out.

Calm down!

Everybody in the taco place is eyeballing you as if you are a screwball and maybe somebody should pick up the phone and call the screwball-restraining people and they'll come to the taco place and sedate you with a couple of shots from a stun gun.

What would your parents think if they see this on News At Eleven?

You being dragged out of the taco place

screaming and hollering hand-cuffed and all.

Please, some decorum.

Remember the plan: All twisted up on the inside, a facial expression of normalcy on the outside. You grip the sides of the table and you are trying to be calm, you really are. But what you really want to do is rip the table from its' foundation and smash it through the plate glass window near the flashing sign that announces: "BUY ONE TACO; GET ONE FREE. FOR A LIMITED TIME ONLY."

Then somehow you're the last customer in the taco place.

I wonder how that could have happened.

And the manager is sweeping up around your feet trying to give you a hint that no matter how deep your misery is, he wants you gone because it's after midnight and he wants to lock up and go because he thinks he's going to get laid by the cashier who just lit her third cigarette since the place closed.

And you're about ready to cry in the taco place because your life has been one big sob story from day one but first you want to bust up the manager's face real good. A broken jaw should do it and get your morale back on the upswing.

One thing not to worry or fret about is this:

Your head doctor will most certainly see you whenever you want. Just pick up the phone and call. This is their business creed and it explains everything: "A screwball on the couch; is money in the bank."

Then about fifteen minutes after midnight this calming aura just transcends all over your body and you don't know where it came from and you know it is not from above because you aren't a spiritual person. And you rationalize that you are in fact a decent person, you really are, and if you can get out of the taco place without busting the manager up, you will be okay and you won't spend a night in jail.

Do this with some degree of decorum.

Just put the crumpled taco wrapping paper and the soda containers in the trash can. Maybe get a damp napkin and wipe the table clean. Tell the manager in a sincere honest voice: "Please excuse my crass behavior, sir. I had a very nice time tonight in your newly opened taco place. The tacos were very good—a little on the spicy side, but still good none-the-less. You have a very nice taco place here and you might see me again if I don't wind up in the nut house for an extended period of time for trying to rip her front door off their damn hinges."

Then just walk out the door, hold your head up high, and don't look back.

On the way back to the dump you live in, twisting, churning, gut wrenching thoughts run through your mind: "Am I the first person to ever have this EYE-DEE-GAFF complex? Am I the first person to ever have this pain and suffering? Where did EYE-DEE-GAFF come from? Who said it first?"

You light a cigarette.

"I'll throw a brick through her window!"

Get yourself stabilized!

Get stabilized!

"What the hell is wrong with me?"

You take a deep drag.

"What did I do to deserve this?"

Enough!

Enough already!

Can't you for one second be honest with yourself and stop wallowing in the mire? Didn't you see this coming? Hasn't she been playing head games with you for months now? It was just last week when you had a date to take her to see a sci-fi movie about virus infected robots taking over the world. And she called you at the last minute and starts mumbling over the phone. She mumbles something about her jaw locking up and she can't talk or chew on popcorn. She further mumbles that the locked jaw would "render me unable to be analytical and properly discuss the film's merits and its' perspective place in cinema history."

Hey guy! You picked her. Real good choice this one.

"Not to worry though," she adds, her voice somehow getting clearer. She tells you she has a friend who is a doctor and he will come over to her place with an x-ray machine and remedy the situation.

Now we know you are not stupid enough to believe this nonsense.

Or maybe you are.

Anyhow, you wanted proof.

Hey! Give her the benefit of the doubt.

So for two hours you park your car outside her front door pretending to be engrossed in a book about the meaning of life.

And not once while you sat there in your rundown car did you see anyone trying to drag an x-ray machine down her miserable street.

There you have it, people have been playing with each other for a long, long time. Want some validation? Just turn on your average life explaining afternoon soap opera and you'll see step by step what people are capable of doing to each other. Many people think this: Soap operas equate to everyday life.

And should they apply to you, pay full attention to the commercials that ask:

"Did you suffer a slip and fall accident?"

You see an old woman with an eastern European accent pointing out cracks in the pavement with the wheels of her walker sobbing at the same time about having her medical coverage terminated.

"Did you get hit by a bus?"

Some poor sucker in a rigid full body cast lying motionless in a hospital bed moans for the camera.

"Are you going through a divorce or bankruptcy?"

The, "we get nothing until you get something" financial solution....

"Then call the Law Offices of ....at........."

Now we all know you're having a hard time getting through everything she did to you, especially giving you the shaft, and we really feel bad for you, but maybe you can take comfort in this.

Right from the door, you were always

decent to her.

You really cared for her, and that's what it's all about.

Didn't you tell her this: "If things are ever going so wrong and you have nowhere else to turn, just pick up the phone and call me."

And just look at what you got for trying to be decent.

Just look at what you got for trying to be a nice guy. You got screwed really good.

Who said EYE-DEE-GAFF first?

Well guy, documented records indicate they had this war somewhere around 966 A. D., and it was over an extra-large-sized piece of green and leafy land with scenic snowcapped mountains about twenty miles off towards the east.

Now in the grand shift of things over years and years, people won't be living on this land any time soon, probably for three hundred years at least, because today it is a fenced in landfill contaminated with nuclear waste located in one of those break-off Soviet Union nations. Back then though it was prime real estate. The dirt was rich black in color and you could grow these special high-carb, energy producing, giant sized potatoes, which were the staff of life and they staved off starvation back then. Through this green and leafy prime potato producing piece of land flowed a great river which brought about quick distribution of product and a huge profit margin.

This was the basic premise for the war.

So these two warring tribes situated east and west of the prime real estate have been going at it for a long time all the while counting the profits they will make upon their victory.

They just wanted an upgrade on their quality of life.

What's wrong with that?

Who could blame them?

They lived like pigs. They wore slaughtered animal skins. They ate raw meat. They never cleansed themselves. Bathroom facilities were deep ditches dug diagonally in the deep woods. And somehow, through all of this, the filth and the slime, they actually pro-created with each other. The result was more fucking idiots running around in slaughtered animal skins.

And as far as we know, there were no head shrinkers available back then to help these screwed up people sort things out.

Now there was a distance problem between the two warring factions. They shot thousands and thousands of arrows at each other. They all fell short. Even their strongest spear chuckers couldn't reach the other side.

You would think that one of the war captains would figure things out and shout out: "Hey! Let's just get closer!"

Then things changed drastically.

Out of nowhere this guy comes along without references, nobody knew where he came from, and he offers to the highest bidder (he wanted half, but the figure was negotiable, of all future profits on the potato industry) a catapulting machine which he guarantees will catapult fire fuck balls to the precise distance needed which will first demoralize, and then bring about complete devastation to the other side.

While setting the distance figuring out dials and then unlocking the catapulting device, the guy starts talking about himself and it's like he's trying to come off as this virtuous person who has morals and is not necessarily after the quick buck.

"I really wanted to invent something, anything, to help all the children. I don't know what I was going to invent, it could be this or it could be that, but as long as it helped the children, that would be inner peace and thanks enough for me."

Why didn't the guy realize he was dealing

with savages and people of this ilk could care less about children or anyone else for that matter?

He continued, "But let's face fucking furious facts here; it's sheer mayhem out there. In this time of turmoil and unrest and uncertainty and the whole world as we know it seems to be blowing apart, I thought I could bring about an end to the chaos by inventing something that would screw up a lot of people real quick which would then bring about hopes for a lasting peace."

He finished with this: "And then we wouldn't need machines of this type."

After a thirty second silent and tense pause:

The first war captain tells his staff: "We're not about to get involved in a bidding war here. Tie him to a tree and use him for target practice. And let's see how this machine works."

The guy was dead on right though.

The fire fuck balls were right on target.

It was sheer havoc on the other side.

Everybody was running around amuck. Stockpiles of slaughtered animal hides were burnt to a crisp. People were getting maimed and messed up. The rear battalion went A.W.O.L. into the deep woods right past the bathroom facilities towards the scenic snowcapped mountains.

So the second war captain, who had a responsibility to nurture and protect and bring culture to the people under his charge, came out from his protective cave during a lull in the incoming fire fuck balls and he made this announcement. "We need volunteers right now! And they should come forward with their battle shields to try to deflect these fire fuck balls. Or else we will all wind up dead and messed up! And I want you to think about our maidens who are young and pure of heart."

Everybody looked at each other and said, "Is he fucking nuts? Let him go out there with a couple of maidens who are young and pure of heart."

The war captain was relentless: "Come forward with your battle shields right now and do as I command! Do you fully realize the sentence that will be imposed on you for dereliction of duty in a declared war? It is death and it won't come easy!"

From the rear, close to where the animal skins were still stacked and smoldering, the strongest spear chucker of them all shouted out at the top of his lungs: "The hell with this! You got us into this! You go out and deal with it!"

And again with utter disgust after throwing

his battle shield towards the deep woods.

"FUCK THIS! I'M GONE FROM HERE!"

The war captain was aghast. A mutiny was building and getting out of control.

"Do you realize the penalty for dereliction of duty in a declared war!?"

Then there was this rising sound that swelled to a roar louder and louder and even louder, then reaching a ground-shaking ear-splitting crescendo.

"EYE-DEE-GAFF!"
"EYE-DEE-GAFF!"
"I WON'T FUCKIN' GO!"
"NO! I WON'T FUCKIN' GO!"

Now let's end things right here.
We've gone far enough.
It just comes down to this.
This is the emotional core of the subject.

It really doesn't matter who won the war of 966 A.D. Who gives a damn about this war anyhow?
This is what counts.

According to the historical records people have been tossing fire fuck balls at each other from the year 966 A.D. up to the present day.

And this is what you should ask yourself.

And really think about your answer.

"How good will I be at deflecting a fire fuck ball if someone tries to toss one at me?"

Little Town Flirt

Bobby Cee, behind his worn out liquor stained bar, working beer taps, muscular upper arms, military buzz haircut, slightly agitated tone to his voice giving *how to act* instructions to a newcomer to his place—a shifty looking character who was eyeballing a sign positioned on the wall. Bobby could read people (a talent he developed after years of running a neighborhood corner bar) and he figured the shifty character was recently released from incarceration probably for retail theft or trying to down payment a used car with a phony check.

He had some basic rules to be followed, Bobby Cee did, if you wanted to hang out in his place and socialize and get to know the local crowd. They weren't too hard to understand. You didn't have to swirl it around in your mind trying to figure out how you were supposed to act while socializing there.

Here's the rules:

- Get drunk; you're flagged.
- No excessive foul language.
- Don't try to borrow money for a drink.

- Run your mouth off and start a fight and you're gone.
- Argue over a game of darts and you're tossed out.
- Other than that; then enjoy yourself here.

The rules were summarized with a black marker on a poster board for a popular brand of beer from out west and it was hung on the wall under a lighting fixture for everyone to see as soon as you walked into the place. The rules were listed under the heading: "Bobby Cee's Rules To Be Here."

Someone still a little dense upstairs?…Just what you might expect in a corner bar, and had trouble figuring the poster board out, then Bobby Cee would verbally summarize it for them using words that were easy to grasp and understand. "I run a nice place here. Just act like you are supposed to act. Okay! And don't act like you're not supposed to act."

One other thing owner and bartender Bobby Cee did was to make sure none of his patrons showed any disrespect whatsoever towards Johnny Marra. Had too much to drink? No excuse. Don't run your mouth off and fuck with Johnny Marra.

This could cause some serious problems for you if you wanted to act like Mr. Tough Guy because Bobby Cee is not the kind of guy you would want to play with. Years ago Bobby was an up-and-coming middleweight from the Tacony section of the city and he had a few professional fights in a rundown fight place in the hard scrapple Kensington section of the City (an automobile accident while changing a flat tire on I-95 southbound ended his dreams) and he could still deliver a devastating left hook that could bust up the side of your face. Besides, you really don't want to try and take on a powerful looking hard-bodied guy with bulging tattooed arms and a military buzz haircut.

These two guys, Bobby Cee and Johnny, go back a long way.

Some of the guys who hung out at *Bobby Cee's Friendly Neighborhood Bar And Grille* heard rumors that Johnny was some kind of a war hero and he received military medals of honor for bravery or getting shot or something else along those lines. But they weren't exactly sure what he received them for or whatever war or conflict he was involved in. It was just understood that you didn't try to bring the subject up to Johnny Marra.

He lost enough over it, enough, you could see it in his eyes, the stone cold dead look inside, and he didn't need any reminders in the form of a dumb question.

Outside *Bobby Cee's Friendly Neighborhood Bar And Grille* in the Frankford section of the city it was bitterly cold. About single digit freezing degrees. It was almost as if you could see four adventurous types weighed down in frigid weather hiking gear wearing thermal boots heading out over Margaret Street on their way to tromp around in the deep woods on the Pocono Mountains about ninety miles north of the city. The sky was midnight black and ominous, as if it would snow at any moment over neighborhood sidewalks attached to narrow row houses making the going home treacherous for anyone leaving the bar after having a few drinks too many.

Some of the blue and yellow bulbs blew out in Bobby's rusted outside hanging sign, others were flickering, no money in the budget for sign repair, and across the street from Bobby's place, a fierce wind whipped through broken windows in upper floors of a long ago closed and boarded up power tool factory.

At the end of their contract years ago, the

union people demanded more and more. The owner took out newspaper ads stating the financial facts for all to see, business was drying up, and unless the union would agree to some concessions and givebacks, the owner would shut the place down and move the factory down south where labor costs are lower without union demands.

Unbelievably, the union shot back:

"NO WAY!"

"NO GIVEBACKS! NO CONCESSIONS!"

"NO CONTRACT! NO WORK!"

"So be it," the third generation owner responded to the union's arrogance. "I've had enough of their demands. I've had enough of their never ending 'Give me more! Give me more!' mindset. I've always tried to be fair to my workers, but these union people just don't get it. It ends now. No more caving in to their demands. Let's just shut it down now and no more dealing with this union nonsense."

The owner shut the factory down within a few months and without any second thoughts moved his factory down south where the labor costs were more cost efficient resulting in a better bottom line for the company. Almost two hundred workers lost their jobs and some union members while collecting unemployment checks lived with the bravado and self-satisfaction that they made no concessions. And it didn't bother the union members at all that their "No Givebacks; No Concessions" mindset screwed their co-workers who wanted to work out of their paychecks.

And these workers, even though most were hard working, had nowhere else to go for employment. Everything started to shift in these jobs. All of the manufacturing jobs from making power tools, television sets and sprinkler heads were now being made in the southern part of the country, or with another developing trend, overseas.

Fierce winds made a howling, almost eerie, sound as they whipped through high up fifth story broken windows. The howling wind may have been a forlorn cry of distress from long ago workers who once made a livable wage and supported their families, mortgaged homes, bought a decent used car and took a few days summer vacation down at the Jersey shore during the factory's seventy-five years in business. Along the cold and barren street and sidewalks littered refuse flew about slightly airborne then making scrapping sounds on the pavement as it landed only to become airborne again.

Johnny Marra sat where he always did, by himself, at the end of the bar with the cork dart board and the dated Music Master juke box just off to his right. Johnny sat there most nights just minding his own business, never bothering anyone, smoking cigarettes, hunched over his drink, mumbling to himself and hearing voices only he could hear. Somehow, just seeing him sitting there by himself, you had the gut feeling that he has seen and been through a lot in his life. Maybe even more than most people have seen, or be expected to see in their entire life, and one more episode might push him over the edge.

Breaking through the mindless chit-chat that goes on in a rundown neighborhood corner bar, someone would drop coins in the jukebox. Maybe something by the Flamingos or the Platters, who knows why a love song by the Flamingos in a place like this?

A song with a dreamy melody, and Johnny, all of a sudden startled, would look around, over his shoulder, wanting with everything inside of him to relive the past, as if he could see himself under dim lighting in a long ago slow dance holding a lover so close, remembering words only lovers say to each

137

other. She would whisper, pulling him closer, "Dance me to the end of making love." Johnny remembered the thrill of it all, could feel his arms embracing her, the stolen kiss and the scent of her jasmine perfume. The excitement knowing there would be passionate love making later on.

Then as the dance sequence in his mind faded out bringing him back to reality realizing the past is done and can't be repeated, Johnny would turn around hunched over his drink mumbling to himself and hearing voices only he could hear.

He would ask himself, maybe just run it through his mind, *what in God's name happened to us? For God's sake, please! Why did this happen?* There is nothing like the emptiness than the total emptiness of someone who has lost everything that ever mattered in his life.

There was one thing different about Johnny tonight after years and years of hanging out in Bobby's place. He was wearing a suit. Who knows why he wore it. It was an expensive looking navy pin-striped suit, and it had seen better days years and years ago. It was rumpled and frayed along the collar and sleeves; it needed dry cleaning, and it was missing some buttons. The white shirt he wore was also rumpled and frayed and it looked like it hadn't been laundered or ironed in some time. When he took his worn out overcoat off, Bobby Cee noticed.

"Hey Guy! Lookin' kind of sharp tonight! Aren't you? Going somewhere special tonight?" Bobby Cee asked, pouring Johnny whiskey. Johnny stood up and struck a somewhat boastful and then a downcast pose. "I got married to a beautiful girl years ago in this suit! Yes I did! What a day it was! And maybe someday soon; they might bury me in it."

"Don't get all dismal and depressed on me now Johnny," Bobby replied in a scolding tone, finishing pouring whiskey in a shot glass. "Think about when you got married wearin' it and what a happy day it was and how lucky you were to get married to such a beautiful girl. Think about that and leave the grim stuff alone. Okay! Remember the good times."

First cousins and postal mailman Lenny and Stubby Stukowski sauntered in, Stubby (he had these short stubby fingers and fat hands) laughing this loud uproarious laugh over some simple-minded joke he told on the way in that Lenny didn't get, but maybe the guys sitting at the bar would figure it out. And they didn't shut the door quick enough allowing a blast of cold air to rush in. Bobby Cee was all over them. "Shut the damn door will ya! You wanna pay for some of the heatin' bill? Times're tough here ya know!"

"Alright! Stop fuckin' yappin' at us! We're customers! Okay!"

They should have left the door opened a little longer, a welcome relief provided from the rush of cold air thinning out somewhat the cigarette haze and the pervasive smell of stale booze.

Stubby got his nickname years ago trying to play in a five-on-five pickup basketball game at the Whitehall Commons Playground on Worth Street situated across the street from the high speed freight and passenger train tracks. He wasn't too good at sports, always being the last one picked. Still he tried crying out: "Throw me the ball! Throw me the ball!" Lenny Blazer side-armed a bullet of a breakaway pass right at Stubby and no one was within twenty feet of him but it went right through his fat hands and stubby fingers hitting him full-impact on the side of his face almost knocking him out.

The first cousins hung up their coats on wall hooks, sat down on swiveling bar stools, rubbed their hands together trying to warm up, tossed cash on the bar, ordered drinks and drank them in greedy swallows. They lit cigarettes and after all that Stubby turned serious after first getting his thoughts together. He just blurted it out, standing up at the same time after downing a shot of whiskey, as if he couldn't wait to say it. He said it loud enough, his eyes flashing, anticipating everyone hanging on his every word and offering their best wishes then sending drinks down his way resulting in a free drinking night for him. Like these guys would give a damn about anything he had to say.

"I'm gettin' married in the spring, yes I am, and I think I wanna!" He expected top shelf stuff sent his way for that statement alone then continuing even after Lenny tried telling him no one gives a damn about what he's saying.

"I think I'm going to marry Ellen Jane. Yeah, I really think so."

What a place to make an announcement like this.

"Are you serious? Where did this come from?" Lenny replied, pausing, then washing his words down with whiskey. A quick agitated drag on his cigarette and more questions. "I mean you haven't known her that long. Have you? Do you love her? You know marriage can last a while, we're talking serious time here. Not an overnight thing. You wanna give up all your freedom?"

Changing his trend of thought for a minute, Lenny yelled at Bobby Cee: "Two more shots here! And make sure you wash the glasses before you pour! No stains on the glasses, okay!"

"Ya want doubles? Do ya?"

"Doubles?......Ya wanna get us plastered? .....We can't shoot darts fucked up!.....and tomorrow......people want their mail don't ya know?"

Stubby looked around pissed off no best wishes and drinks coming his way and "screw it!" now pays for his drinks.

Stubby answered the marital related freedom question.

"Yeah! Yeah I think so." Then nodding his head aggressively.

"You think so! Are you fuckin' crazy?"

"Well look at it this way. At least I'll get laid every night and our love will come from that. The more you do it the more in love you get. That's what I heard about it. Sounds about right to me. Everyone says that and it makes sense. It's just basic common sense, that's all! There's no figurin'

142

out needed."

Lenny's thinking, *what the hell did I just hear?*

Three stools over by the door, Bobby poured two shots and a beer for Hank, the retired fireman who lives row-housed on the 4500 block of Melrose Street. "Two bucks Hank! Pay up! That's the good stuff."

Stubby's cousin just sat there for a minute, bewildered in his mindset, trying to sort out everything he just heard. He had this look on his face as if he was in deep thought just waiting for some profound words to come to him that he could say in response. After a drag on his cigarette this: "Why not! Give it a shot! Whadda you got to lose? And every night you get laid!"

There was hardly anyone in the place. And it's been that way ever since the power tool factory shut down years ago, bringing to an end workers coming in to unwind and booze it up at the end of their work shifts. Years ago things were on the upside. On weekend nights Bobby would have neighbor, fifty year old Johnny Rhome, playing guitar and singing bar songs on a small stage and the neighborhood row house crowd would come in for some drinks and sing along musical entertainment.

Just then, while the first cousins were still discussing marriage and getting laid, the outsider to the place, the shifty looking newcomer, thinking he wouldn't be noticed with serious conversation going on tried to snatch Stubby's postal delivery jacket from a hook on the wall and abscond with it out through the door into the cold black night. Hank the retired fireman from Melrose Street noticed the heist going down and he aggressively stopped the culprit at the door with his meat hook hands. Hank jacked him up against the wall by his throat, and jacked up against the wall the culprit's legs started twitching.

Hank retrieved the jacket and tossed it towards Stubby. He threw the guy out the door and after he bounced off the frozen pavement, Hank issued a threat: "You come round here again and we'll beat the livin' piss outta you!" Stubby showing his appreciation sent a top shelf drink Hank's way. Now that's real corner bar protocol in action.

Bobby Cee had enough of another long and unproductive day and he didn't want to hang around any longer for just a few more bucks in the cash register. Over an hour before closing time, he announced wearily while lighting his last cigarette,

""Last Call! One more drink and that's it for the night! I've had enough! It's time to go home."

One of the cousins, it was probably Stubby Stukowski, he was prone to shooting off his mouth, shouted out really agitated standing up for dramatic effect: "What the fuck ya mean?...Whatta ya...mean.. Closin' up! We just got here a while ago. We wanna shoot some darts! Besides! Somebody's getting married. We wanna celebrate! And besides, nobody said best wishes and here's a drink on me!" Lenny tried to jerk him down on his bar stool but Stubby slipped his grip.

Bobby didn't want to hear any bullshit, but then on second thought, he acquiesced, feeling a little celebration was due. After all, for as long as he could remember, no one ever announced he was getting married after downing a shot and a beer in his place. "Okay! A free shot of whiskey for whoever's getting married. But we're still closing. up!"

For quite some time Bobby's had aspirations wanting to get out of the run-down bar business growing weary of it. He's been eyeballing this vacant oversized clothing store on Frankford Avenue with the idea of selling the bar and opening a pool hall. And for convenience sake there is a second floor apartment so he could be close to his new business to make sure no one tries to break in the middle of the night while the pool hall is closed.

An announcement from Stubby after he downed Bobby's getting married gesture and he banged his empty shot glass on the bar for dramatic effect. "Ya see what's happened here! Common courtesy that's what it is. Ya say you're getting married, send down to the person getting married a drink. It's common courtesy the way it is. What's it cost to send a drink? A buck?"

The Stukowski cousins heard the rumors about Bobby's ability to deliver a punishing left hook so being a little intimidated, they figured out it's best to just let things go, reasoning that they'll come back and shoot darts and celebrate another night.

"I've had it with this day. It's over! See ya tomorrow." Bobby Cee told the Stukowski cousins, and everyone else in the place, then rinsing glasses out and wiping up cigarette ash and liquor stains from the bar.

Hearing Bobby's last call announcement, it was like something went off in Johnny Marra. Something just clicked in his head. For as long as anyone could remember, Johnny would just sit there hardly ever saying anything. Then out of nowhere, in the glare of some orange tinted light from a hanging beer sign exclaiming the use of crystal clear spring water and barley hops wearing his rumpled suit, he announced: "One more for me!" Johnny exclaimed. "Yes! One more for me! Three fingers in a tall glass please!"

Bobby Cee poured whiskey slowly in a tall glass asking Johnny at the same time if he was alright. "Yeah, I'm okay!" Johnny boasted standing up his glass held high aloft for all to see. "Yes I'm okay! Damn, yes I am! And I propose a toast to myself! Yes I do! A toast to myself! A toast to me, Johnny Marra! Johnny Marra from Tacony! Hooray for Johnny!"

Bobby Cee's trying to shut his place down, and Johnny Marra's coming alive. His voice was suddenly clear and vibrant and Johnny didn't have to steady himself grabbing on to the bar while his other hand held his glass high aloft. Shooting darts by himself, Reggie the *Big Cad*, the neighborhood big mouth, just couldn't keep his mouth shut while letting a dart fly. But he has been this way his whole life with his big mouth. "Finally, Johnny's gone nuts!" Bobby Cee told Reggie the *Big Cad* to shut the fuck up.

"A toast to me! A wonderful lover!"

Still holding his glass high aloft, Johnny's hand trembled slightly.

A man's soliloquy in the spotlight about the love of his life.

"Yes me! A wonderful lover! And Mary and me, we were connected to the stars once. And she said I was a wonderful lover. And I loved her so much. More than anything in the world, that's how much I loved her. And she was mine and I couldn't stand being without her."

Reggie the *Big Cad* probably would have tried to open his big mouth again (or maybe not, maybe he got caught up in the moment) if it wasn't for the fact that Bobby Cee was glaring at him. Unaware of what was going on with Johnny Marra, Richie *Slave Driver* Shumaker, half-fucked up at the other end of the bar, was running his mouth off to anyone who would listen, cigarette dangling from the corner of his mouth while pointing to his jaw, stating fiercely that he could withstand being cold cocked to the jaw without being knocked unconscious. This just your typical neighborhood barroom talk from someone who's half-tanked up.

"Go ahead! Anyone! Try and cold cock me! See if I drop!"

Johnny Marra is baring his heart and soul for all to see and hear about the love of his life, and *Slave Driver*, at the other end of the bar, is challenging anyone to cold cock him to the jaw exclaiming the punch wouldn't knock him out.

"Go ahead! Fuckin' punch me! Right here," pointing to his jaw.

Slave Driver's seizure dog, Slasher, sat by his feet begging for packaged sausage sticks his tail whomping back and forth: "Woof! Woof! Woof!" He needed the seizure dog, *Slave Driver* did, after taking a few too many shots to his jaw bringing on seizure attacks out of nowhere. Slasher, ever loyal the seizure dog, if a seizure took place, would remain by his master's side, "Woof! Woof! Woof!" until help would arrive.

Johnny sat back down the exuberance in his voice drifting away. "You sure you're okay, Johnny?" Bobby Cee asked, concern in his voice about his life-long friend, setting the whiskey bottle down on the bar smeared with liquor stains and cigarette ash that hadn't been wiped clean yet.

Johnny went on, his voice above a whisper. "Look at me now will ya. I'm all fucked up."
"How did things get so screwed up?"

Reggie *the Big Cad* let another dart fly.

"I lost everything. I lost her."

"I should have died out there."

Slave Driver's still pointing at his chin. Slurring mindless words.

"They should've just left me out there."

"Where was God when I needed him?"

Johnny took out pictures from his coat pocket…a strip of four black and white photos from a seashore arcade photo booth taken years ago. Johnny looked at the pictures for at least the ten-thousandth time. Something came over him. Him and his Mary. They looked so perfect together. So young and so happy and so long ago.

The pictures were wrinkled and yellowed at the edges. He choked up a bit looking at them, and it was as if in his mind at least, that Johnny could go back to the sun lit day and the photo booth when the pictures were taken. He remembers telling Mary, "Let's go in and hold hands and strike a pose then we'll have pictures showing what a happy couple we are."

Slave Driver on his way out, Slasher following, slurring words back into the place. "I was in the spotlight once! Yes I was! I 'member when I won stock car races at the Vineland Drag Strip and was in the winner's circle somewhere in New

Jersey over the bridge in N. J." Trying to sort out in his mind the details as to how he wound up in the winner's circle over the bridge in Vineland, *Slave Driver* walked towards home over James Street, Slasher at his side matching his master's steps.

Years ago when he was younger and not too bright, *Slave Driver* somehow inherited a significant amount of cash. With some of the cash he bought a 409 cubic inch powered midnight black two-door hardtop. The car had a posi-traction rear, dual exhaust, four barrel carb and four on the floor. The August day was dry and perfect for drag racing but somehow *Slave Driver* lost control of the 409 powered hardtop and...BAM!!!...he sideswiped and flipped over after careening into the concrete retaining barrier at a high rate of speed at the one-point-two-five mileage marker.

The rescue squad needed jaws-of-life to extract *Slave Driver* from the crumpled wreck. He was banged up and bruised, lumps on his forehead, cuts here and there, some needing stitching up, and he was woozed out walking in semi-circles. *Slave Driver* was asking this, wanting to make sure his question was indeed the fact. "Am I really in the Winner's Circle?"

It's hard to fault *Slave Driver*, after all, it was

his first race.

He mumbled through swollen lips, "Should I make a victory speech? Where's the trophy?"

Voices behind the barrier exalted, "We've seen a miracle here. He lives to race another day!"

Dimly lit, a little after one a.m., the place was empty now. Cigarette haze hovering aloft. Just two friends sitting at the bar. Bobby Cee turned most of the lights off. Johnny asked a favor of his friend. "I have to do something soon, but I don't think I have the courage to do it by myself. But if you let me have one of those bottles, I might find the courage to do it. Just help me out on this, please." Bobby told him, "Anything for a friend."

Bobby wanted to suggest praying as a means to perhaps in some way to ease his inner torment but he knew Johnny gave up on that a long time ago. He tried anyhow.

"Prayers! Are you joking? All I wanted to do is come home in one piece to my wife. Do you know what it's like to lose everything? My wife, my ability to work a decent job. I have nothing. I lost everything. I wouldn't waste ten seconds on a prayer. Let the fools pray. Let them have their false hopes."

Things were golden for Johnny years ago

when he was twenty-two years old and handsome and some people thought he had a striking resemblance to movie icon, James Dean. Johnny was into sports in high school and he received a partial scholarship to a small college in South Carolina, but he shrugged it off, deciding that college just wasn't for him. Working with his hands was what he wanted to do, and for Johnny, it was a sign of manhood.

Making his Dad real proud, Johnny accepted an apprentice plumbing position at the Philadelphia Navy Yard in South Philadelphia. Johnny's father was proud that his son was following in his footsteps. The Marra family, along with the extended Marra family, was blue collar all the way.

Before he started his apprenticeship, Johnny worked as a furniture mover which bulked up the muscles on his athletic frame. He was in the prime years of his physical prowess. Johnny didn't take any gruff from anyone who would try to get up in his face. He had this cocky, go ahead and try to play with me attitude about himself, but he was never known for starting any nonsense. With the money he saved during the years he worked in the furniture moving business, before he started his apprenticeship position, Johnny bought his first car—a used low slung sport's convertible. A car with some flash and roar—a head turning machine—that's what he wanted.

So just about everything is going right for Johnny.

He's young and he's handsome and his future looks bright.

He was an only child and his parents thought the world of him.

And then he met her. And things got even better.

He's hanging out with his friends outside *Chink's Steak and Hoagie Shop* on Sheffield Avenue in the Northeast section of the city. It was a time when some of the best friends you ever had in your life were there with you just hanging out on a corner in the neighborhood.

Leaning against his sport's car, leaving his radio on tuned to the hot hits station, he's talking to his friend Bobby Cee about his car, and then after lighting a cigarette and his mood changing downward about getting dumped by some girl he was seeing. Johnny tells Bobby he's tired of being strung along by girls who do nothing but play mind games with you telling you you're the only one for them and then just like that they just ditch you for somebody else.

Johnny laments, "It's like that song you hear on the Solid Gold Station about making sure your heart is strong when you start seeing some girls because they're the kind that can wind up giving you the boot out the door."

With a high energy radio Dee Jay announcing a top ten hit song about finding summer love, Bobby Cee agrees with Johnny.

"They can be a bitch playing with your head like that. They can really put the screws to you. But then you see something built really nice with great legs and you say to yourself, 'I'd really like to get close to her." Bobby lights a cigarette, looks dismayed, and he asks, "What're you going to do?"

Bobby adds, "I would just like to have a dance by chance with some beautiful thing, blue eyes and blond hair and all that. It might go like this, a great love song playing and I would go over to her and ask her if by chance I could have the next dance with her. And I would hold her so close. And nothing else would matter, just me and her slow dancing to this beautiful love song. And I would tell her ever so softly, 'I feel like I am the luckiest guy in the world holding you this close.' I just hope one day I find love or love comes to me."

Shrugging his shoulders, Johnny offers aspirations. "I'd just like to meet a girl who isn't a little town flirt. You know the type. First she tells you she cares for you and she wants to be with you and she makes these promises and just like that she's got her eyes on some other guy telling you at the same time that she doesn't want to be tied down to anyone." Johnny pauses, looks up and down the avenue, and he adds, "I shouldn't be hanging on the corner like this. Somehow....I should be somewhere with someone."

Reggie the *Big Cad* comes out of Chink's wolfing down a cheese steak drenched with tomato sauce as if someone might try to snatch it right out of his hands and catching the drift of Johnny's conversation he adds this after wiping sauce from his mouth with the back of his hand. "As soon as they start playing with you, get the fuck out. Don't stay around for the pain. Don't get your balls busted just because you're trying to get a feel job."

Shaking his head side to side, Bobby Cee looks amazed by what he's just heard. He says, "You know what Reggie? You sound like a real head shrinker. You should buy a leather couch and open an office for screwballs."

Leaning against Chink's store front glass, Little Joe and Walt Barookie are in discussion about where they could go to pick up some girls and maybe get lucky. Lucky back then meant maybe getting a phone number that wasn't fake. Little Joe suggests trying the *El Rancho Drive In Western Style Restaurant* on Frankford Avenue and maybe they can hit on the waitresses who come out to your car to take your order on roller skates. Figuring things out, Walt Barookie says: "We 'aint picked anything up there yet. Let's go downtown and see if anything's strutting around down there."

Sonny *the Sandwich Maker* comes out and yells, "Get off the window glass. Okay! You might bust it and who pays for it then? And yo! Reggie, you short- changed me on the cheese steak. Pay up! Okay! Fifty cents!"

"Whadda ya mean? Accusing me of short changing you!" Reggie the *Big Cad* bellows between bites on his cheese steak drenched with sauce.

So, it's hot and ninety-two degrees outside.

Sonny *the Sandwich Maker* wants Reggie *the Big Cad* to cough up some cash.

Reggie *the Big Cad*'s talking like a head shrinker.

Little Joe says, "Okay, let's go downtown."

Johnny clicks off his car radio wanting to conserve battery energy.

Before driving off downtown, Little Joe exclaims, "Hope we get lucky!"

Bobby Cee's still talking about how some girls can put the screws to you.

And out of the corner of his eye Johnny Marra sees her walking in the sunlight down the avenue towards *Chink's Steak and Hoagie Shop.*

He can hardly believe what he sees. He thinks some heavenly creature was sent down from above to walk down Sheffield Avenue towards him for only him to see. She is just so out-and-out pretty. She looks so beautiful in her beige summer dress her shapely legs coming out from it very nicely. He can't help but notice her blond hair and intelligent blue eyes as she walks by directly in his field of vision. Johnny and Bobby in awe of her beauty stepped back towards the red convertible to give her more room to walk on by them.

Salvation for Johnny? Salvation from hanging on the corner?

Still leaning against his red low-slung sport's car, Johnny's just stunned, almost unable to move, thinking to himself, *God! Who is she? She's beautiful. Where did she come from?* He wanted to say something but the words wouldn't come out.

Bobby Cee couldn't help but notice the expression on Johnny's face and it's almost as if he's in some kind of a trance and maybe somebody should try and snap him out of it but it looks like he's too far gone.

Then, some encouragement.

"Johnny! Yo Johnny! Go ahead! Take a shot at her! Whatta you got to lose? Try and get her phone number, why don't you?" Bobby Cee exclaims, encouraging him, slightly pushing him in the direction she's walking.

Ever the big mouth, Reggie the *Big Cad* pontificates, "Don't waste your time! I tried to hit on her and she didn't give me the time of day. Must be something wrong with her. She must be one of those frigid types. You know! She thinks she's too good for anyone."

More encouragement.

Bobby shoves Johnny again. "Go ahead! Go! Give it a shot!"

Thinking about what he was going to say to her taking deep breaths breathing air he didn't breathe before, Johnny tried to shake the negative thoughts he was having about himself not being good enough to talk to her. He remembered his mother's words always telling him, "If you have negative thoughts; you will get negative results. Always think positive." Johnny caught up with her around the corner from *Chink's Steak and Hoagie Shop* along tree lined Devereaux Avenue in front of *Vince's Barber Shop,* just across the street from the neighborhood playground.

Mary Denali told her friends she gave him a try because he seemed honest and sincere, he was handsome, and he didn't try to give her the same worn out hackneyed pick-up lines she's heard over and over again when they first spoke on Devereaux Avenue. Worn out lines like the one Reggie *the Big Cad* tried on her, "What's a beautiful thing like you walking around here all by yourself? You could use some company."

He couldn't have said it any better. It's like he picked up the words from a movie or a passage in a book or something else along those lines.

"Hi! My name's Johnny. And I think if you would just give me a few hours out of one of your days, we would have a nice time together. And it would be nice to get to know you. Please, give me a try. Just a few hours out of one of your days."

Things can change so quickly when you

don't even expect it. One minute Johnny's lamenting about getting the boot from some girl, and the next minute he's talking to this beautiful thing. What a turnaround within a few minutes and the day now seemed full of promise.

From that moment on, across the street from the neighborhood playground, on the pavement along Devereaux Avenue outside *Vince's Barber Shop*, they both seemed to just hit it off together.

"Hi Johnny! My name's Mary. It's so nice to meet you."

It wasn't love at first sight, but maybe something close to it.

On their first date, Johnny got Mary home around midnight. If he could, he told her, he would start the day all over again. He remembers it as if it just happened yesterday. He runs it through his mind again and again. Johnny got up real early that Saturday morning. He washed and polished his red sport's car in front of his Tacony neighborhood row house.

The guys on the corner heard of Johnny's plans for the day and they were envious. Johnny with a beautiful girl by his side in his low slung convertible music playing on the loud side heading towards the Jersey shore. And they're doing nothing but hanging on the corner. Reggie *the Big Cad* was out-and-out jealous.

He picked Mary up at her home on Algard Street. He met her parents and he felt nervous about the mandatory opening chit-chat and what he was going to say; everything went okay with that. Mary's parents were impressed hearing Johnny talk about his prospects for the future. Then they drove over the Tacony Palmyra Bridge and headed south towards the Wildwoods down at the New Jersey shore. It was a perfect summer day. With the radio playing on the loud side tuned to the hot hits station with the convertible top down, Johnny drove over the back roads avoiding the boring New Jersey highways. Mary said she loved driving through the sunshine with the wind blowing through her hair.

Walking hand in hand at the ocean's edge, Johnny told Mary he was so happy just to be with her. She told him being down the Jersey shore was one of her favorite places and she was glad to share it with him. Early in the evening along the boardwalk, the bright flashing lights exhilarated both of them. They laughed together trying to win at arcade games with pitchmen hawking cheap prizes.

At an open air pavilion a free concert was

given by a local band playing popular hit songs, and they danced just about every dance, especially the slow ones with Johnny holding Mary close.

"We fit into each other's arms perfectly," Johnny whispered to Mary slow dancing to a song about summer love with a full moon high above. There was something magical about the moment when Johnny took Mary into his arms for the first time. He wanted the dance to last forever. It was a perfect summer evening.

Conversation came easy on the way home driving through the cool summer night and before they knew it they were back in the city that felt lifeless and without either one of them saying it, they both wished they could turn the car around and go back to where they came from. Feeling really good about the day, and with stars shinning high above, Johnny kissed Mary a goodnight kiss he wished would never end. Mary didn't resist. He told her he couldn't wait to see her again. Mary didn't say anything, but she felt the same. From that day on, all Johnny wanted to do was to be with Mary. When he was with her, everything was right and he didn't have a care in the world. One thing Johnny felt that eased his mind was that Mary wasn't a little town flirt playing any kind of mind games.

A few months later, Mary told her parents with Johnny she found a nice guy she thinks she could marry one day. "When I'm with him it's like I get the chills. I get this funny feeling all over. There must be something to it."

As time went on, Johnny and Mary's families got to know each other and there was talk that a wedding could take place in the future. Both families exclaimed how happy the couple looked whenever they were together.

"Picture perfect together," Mary's sister, Connie, exclaimed camera in hand taking snap-shots at a family get together. Next summer Connie married her high school sweetheart and at the wedding reception a feeling came over Johnny and Mary as to what they both wanted in the future. They knew they wanted to spend their lives together and nothing else would matter.

Then things started to unravel and it came from an outside source that was beyond their control. Johnny received official government notification that he had to fulfill his military obligation and he had thirty days until he had to report for basic training.

It was a time when young men were faced

with a mandatory military obligation, unless you were privileged being in college and received a deferment, and the fear was you would be sent to some god-forsaken jungle on the other side of the world and you would come home severely maimed, or worse yet, mothers and fathers feared their sons would come home in a flag-draped military coffin.

Mary was devastated but she hid her feelings from Johnny. No matter what, she would be strong for him.

Johnny's mind was all tangled up and he was going off in ten different directions at once. Everything seemed so right to him and now things are falling apart. The strength Johnny felt he would need to get through this would come if he and Mary were married. He knew in his heart he could get through anything with her by his side for all days to come.

Johnny let his feelings out with Mary. Rivers and rivers of them. He told her how much he loved her and with her by his side everything would work out for all days to come. They were at their favorite place, down at the New Jersey shore. Walking along the ocean's edge Johnny's mind was racing thinking how he could ask her what was really on his mind. He had a hard time hiding his feelings and Mary sensed what was coming next. On the drive down, Johnny was acting all edgy and nervous and he was groping for things to say.

He just stopped in the brilliant sunshine. People all around. He took a deep breath. This was a moment that could change his life. Taking her hand in his he got the words out. "Would you please marry me? I will love you and treasure you for all the days of my life. You are all that I need and nothing could ever happen to us as long as we are together. Please, marry me."

It was as if time stood still for him at that moment. Mary felt as if they were the only two people on the crowded beach. They only saw each other.

She answered, "Yes!" and a feeling of sheer happiness swept over him and he knew in his heart that everything would be okay for all days to come.

She held him close. "I love you so much. You are all that I want. I will always be by your side. No matter what we would ever be faced with, I would never leave you. I would never leave you. We will always be together, you and me. Always and forever."

It was as if the things they told each other hovered above them and if anyone in the future should pass under them they would somehow feel the love Johnny and Mary had for each other.

They made love that afternoon, passionate love, in a motel complex overlooking the boardwalk and the ocean. The kind of love young people in the prime of their lives can make. At the height of her passion, holding Johnny so close in her arms, she gasped, "You're a wonderful lover Johnny! Yes you are! A wonderful lover! I love you so much!" He remembered her words for the rest of his life.

Their parents were against their hasty wedding plans feeling they were being made under the duress of Johnny fulfilling his military obligation in troubling times. "Why don't you wait? Give it some time," they implored.

They told their parents: "We are not waiting. We are too much in love." Their families relented realizing how much they loved each other. Their wedding was small, in a chapel just off the main altar of Mary's church. Only a few people attended, just family members and a few close friends. There was no time for an elaborate ceremony. Knowing full well what this couple was going through, first the joy and happiness of their marriage, then the uncertainty of Johnny going off to fulfill his military obligation, the priest said a silent prayer to himself.

Please God. Watch over him and bring him home safe and sound to his wife and family.

Time went by fast after their wedding. Together they faced a day they hoped would never come. Time slowed only when they were in each other's arms making love. They had a last weekend together staying in a high rise hotel in the downtown section of the city. During the day they walked around hand in hand trying to enjoy downtown as best they could. Late at night they sat on a roof top deck and they wished they could just escape to another place. A place where they could be free of all of this. All they wanted was to be together. Mary looked up and said, "Johnny, look up at the stars in the heavens. Look up at the stars while you are away and I will to. And we will be connected by the stars until you come home."

Platform 4 E, lower level, of the Center City East Rail Station was crowded with military inductees and family and friends waiting on a train they hoped would never come. Silent prayers swept through all of this. Prayers for a safe return of their loved one. Slowly coming into the station a silver-streaked passenger train bringing with it a silence to the train station. Johnny held Mary close. He told her, "I will come home to you and nothing will ever come between us again." Mary tried to keep her emotions under control. "I will always be here for you. Remember that always, no matter how far away from me you are."

Mary held back tears while kissing him goodbye. Johnny stood at the rear door of the last car of the southbound train. As the train pulled away Mary seemed smaller and smaller almost like a dot at the end of the station. The train picked up speed and Mary seemed to blend in with all the other dots along the platform. When the train escaped from the railroad tunnel into the brilliant sunshine, Johnny never felt so alone in his life.

Nine months later, from some god forsaken place on the other side of the world, he wrote a letter to his best friend, Bobby Cee.

Hey Bobby,

You have to promise me something. Don't let me down. Got to hold you to this. No maybes. Don't ever tell Mary what I tell you about this place. I don't want her worried and last thing I don't want her upset.

It's scary here. Damn scary this god forsaken place. Best way I can describe it there's a smell of death about it. I've seen death and it's like you breathe it in. I've seen legs blown off and bodies blown apart. And you see this and you can't even think straight your head's so screwed up. Then the nightmares come. You don't know where the enemy is, could be anywhere.

Trying to hold on. I get high once in a while, you have to if you want to block out the fear, and the fear is always there, and I count the days till I'm gone from here. I'll tell you, you breathe in the fear. I pray to God I make it. I just want to be with Mary. That's what keeps me sane, thinking about being with her again. I've seen too much here. Don't think you can recover from this. How can anyone? I'll live with this forever.

I'll write again, say some prayers for me. Johnny

P.S. Anything happens to me here, tell Mary how much I loved her.

It was a dangerous operation rumored to come. Orders came down from Headquarters. Echo Platoon, Bravo Company Infantry Division was ordered out for a search and destroy mission in the middle of a sultry night.

Fear levels were rising. Air support was to be called in if the enemy they encountered was in large numbers. Two short-timers with only a week to go were taken off the mission. They survived their year of duty and respect was shown in that they would be going home to their loved ones.

Johnny geared up. Everything he needed for battle: M-16 Rifle plus 6 ammo packs, 4 grenades, hand held flares, a small arms pistol, a packed rucksack and 2 canteens of water. He took fear with him also. Leaving the base camp Johnny fell in behind and to the right of the point man. They passed a 200 yard open security area avoiding buried claymore mines and camouflaged razor wire and then the foliage and the sultry night air quickly enveloped Echo Platoon.

A hard rain started to fall. Johnny's running things Mary told him through his mind hoping they could take him to another place. Anyplace that was close to Mary even if it was only in his mind.

"You're a wonderful lover, Johnny."

The strap of his M-16 dug into his shoulder.

"We are connected by the stars."

Enemy fire could come from anywhere.

"I will always love you and I would never leave you."

Ahead an opening from the foliage, easy targets out in the open.

Then he prayed out in the open. "Our Father who art in……" Johnny couldn't get another word out. All fuckin' hell broke loose. Point man, Paul Gallo, cries out, "Jesus Christ…….I'm hit!" Droplets of blood from Paul Gallo's neck wound sprays back on Johnny. Enemy flares light up the area providing easy targets. Fear grips Echo platoon. His heart racing, Johnny dives for cover. Anywhere. Before he hits the ground, the bullet tears through his shoulder. Searing pain shoots through his body. Machine gun fire came from everywhere. Tracer bullets hissed overhead.

Radio telephone operator screamed into his device. Panic in his voice. "Red Alert! Fuckin' Red Alert!…. We're Lit up! Repeat Lit Up!…. Guys Zapped! Need Air Support! Need Medevac! Now! Now! Now!"

Johnny slammed into a ditch. He saw his blood flowing down his arm mixing with water in the ditch turning it crimson red in color. He looked up and saw the heavens and he cried out, "God please don't let me die like this! Don't let me die here! Please let me go home to my wife! God Save me!" He heard the screams of the wounded and the dying. Johnny saw the stars above, he felt connected to his Mary.

Then salvation from the slaughter. Air support and rescue helicopters.

"Stay with me soldier! Don't you die on me damn it! You're gonna make it!" A medic implored on the helicopter lifting him away from the carnage below. "You got someone waiting for you at home soldier?"

"I do. My wife. My Mary." Then everything goes black.

After an extensive stay at a military hospital, recovery came slowly. He came home to his Mary on a cold bleak day, the direct opposite of the summer day he left her. They fell into each other's arms.

Fear came over Mary. From deep inside her she sensed that this was not the same Johnny who left her on a brilliant summer day. All of the good things Johnny had going for him before he left for military service fell apart when he came home. Injuries to his shoulder prevented him from starting his plumbing apprenticeship. He worked a series of low-end jobs working as hard as he could. Each one just fell apart. Johnny was trying his best so him and Mary could start their lives together. Their parents were devastated.

Then some hope for a job with a future.

Johnny's father-in-law helped him attain an entry position in the main office of a local savings and loan association. Mary was elated, some hope for the future. Things didn't work out too well. He couldn't concentrate. He kept having on the job battlefield flashbacks. He heard the screams. Supervisors were hesitant on giving him assignments because he was easily startled. After three months they had to let him go.

His marriage went on a downward spiral. He felt detached and anxious and he couldn't sleep because the nightmares of what he saw kept waking him up. Help and counseling was available but the best in their field couldn't reach him. Johnny told them, "You don't know what it's like. These flashbacks and I hear the screams. I feel the bullet tearing through my shoulder. I see myself in the ditch, blood pouring out of me and the dead bodies around me. I don't know what it is. I feel like I don't even know my wife. It's like she is a stranger to me. Somebody far away I can't reach. This is sheer fucking hell I'm going through. I can't even hold a job. I feel like I'm losing everything."

His wife pleaded, "Please Johnny come back to me. I love you! I need you! Without you there is nothing." God, she tried to make it work.

God did she try. She worked two jobs to help pay the bills. Mary prayed and prayed. She tried until she just couldn't take it anymore. It was seeing her Johnny on an never-ending downward spiral that finally broke her spirit.

She left him on a summer day. Mary was only 28 years old and she lived through so much in the five years since Johnny came home from military service. Anything she could do to bring him back to her she tried. Anything. It wasn't in her heart to look back when she walked away. She couldn't take seeing Johnny watch her walk away.

But she remembered this:
The day when Johnny caught up with her around the corner from *Chink's Steak and Hoagie Shop* and he said this to her, "Hi! My name's Johnny. And I think if you would give me a few hours out of one of your days, we would have a nice time together. And it would be so nice to get to know you. Please, give me a try. Just a few hours out of one of your days."

With everything inside her, she wished it could happen again.

Johnny Marra walked home from Bobby Cee's neighborhood bar though the cold black night. He drew his coat collar up against the frigid night air. He walked underneath the trash littered railroad bridge supported by large grimy stone blocks on each side of Margaret Street. He dug his right hand deep into his coat pocket and he felt something. He pulled out a strip of pictures taken years ago on a golden day in a seashore arcade photo booth. Johnny looked at them one last time and he crumpled them up and he tossed them on the windswept trash littered pavement.

Against the howling wind he walked up the steep incline on Trenton Street to his second floor apartment overlooking the high speed railroad corridor. His evil demons followed him clawing at him, ripping his soul apart, always there to remind him of everything he has lost. Sitting on the edge of his bed he drank from the bottle his friend Bobby Cee gave him to help build up his courage, evil demons alongside him, hissing at him.....Hissing. *Go ahead! Do it! It's the last thing you have to do!*. A high-speed freight train roared by causing his frost covered bedroom windows to shudder.

Johnny may have prayed. He had rosary beads clutched tight around his fingers. A hand-written note in black ink was found on his bureau. The note read, "I look up at the stars now and then and I no longer feel a connection to her. All is lost forever." From his bureau drawer he took out a silver plated pistol and with a large caliber bullet in its chamber he shot himself through the base of his brain.

Twin Brother Stories

"I almost caught that sucker."
"I wish I had another shot at it. "
Bill "*Tiger*" Stukowski

Got my feathers trimmed last week. I went to *Vince's Friendly Neighborhood Barber Shop* on Torresdale Avenue. Twelve bucks ain't bad. The barber shop has been in the same location, just down the avenue from the playground and the discount tire garage, for over sixty years.

Vince's father, Dominic, started the business and he raised six kids cutting hair. Vince grew up in the business and he took over when his father retired. Actually, Vince wanted no part of cutting hair when he was younger. He had his dreams, anything other than being a barber. But his father implored him, "Vincent! You're the youngest. You're the smartest. Your brothers, especially Carlo, aren't too bright. Can you imagine? Carlo wants to start a car crushing and salvage business. What's wrong with him? Who will I turn this gold mine over to? Who? Your sisters can't take it; they're all married with kids. I can't believe that Roseann has five kids already and she's not even thirty years old and she's married to a lazy bum."

So I'm sitting there kind of relaxing—I've been a little tense lately—waiting my turn reading supermarket tabloids, which I never read unless I'm in Vince's waiting to get my feathers trimmed. I have to admit that I've been a little tense lately. They're downsizing at work. My 401K is going down the shaft. And this past weekend over an expensive dinner at a chic restaurant my almost-fiancée (I almost asked her to marry me six months ago) told me she wants to take her French lessons to the next level so she says she's moving to France for six months.

Outside of this, everything is grand.

Vince's place, by the way, is not even close to being a high-end upscale hair cutting salon with a receptionist at the front desk where you need to make an appointment to get even a basic haircut with a price tag of forty or fifty bucks plus a tip. I'm seated next to an old bathroom sink now filled with wilting plants. I overhear Vince telling Ren Davis, the neighborhood insurance agent, that he would like to open a shop in Olde City so that he could attract the upper class high society crowd.

Vince told Ren he's thinking about calling his new place *Scissors For The Elite.* "Who knows," Vince said, cutting away, "maybe I'll get some celebrities and main liners in there and maybe I'll get on someone's guest list for an upper-crust high-society soiree."

Vince's barber shop radio had the oldies' station on and the *Your Request Hour* just started, and some of that stuff just drives me nuts. These people have heard these songs thousands and thousands of times over the past forty years or so and they still have to hear them one more time. So they call in, again and again.

"Hello! This is Angie from South Philly. I can't remember the name of the song, it's been so long, but the words are about a church in a city and the bells are always ringing and never stopping and couples are going through the deep woods to get to the canyons to get rejuvenated. Can you play it for me?"

The Dee Jay responds with his high energy radio voice, "Sure we can, Angie. Do you want to dedicate the song to anyone?" Angie gushes back.

"Oh Yes! I wanna dedicate it to my husband, Salvatore. We met in a canyon out west during the eighties and he was completely stoned out of his mind and he was staggering around and I was sight-seeing there. I gotta admit I was a little high myself, just a joint or two, but that was it. But after years of therapy, we had an okay life together. But last week he overdosed and we're praying for him and maybe if he hears this song he'll think back and realize the days in the canyon weren't too good for him."

Ren tells Vince, "If you open your shop in Olde City and get some famous people in there, let me know, get me some leads, maybe I can sell them some insurance."

Vince looks my way over the partition between the barber chairs and the waiting area. "You're next, Ron. Hey, is that the issue something about the Zombie or mummy they caught or they're looking for somewhere?"

I'm embarrassed to answer being caught reading this junk, "Zombie....Being caught? I haven't got to that part yet."

"I think it's on page one," Vince instructed. "There's pictures."

I picked up the expression about getting my feathers trimmed from an old friend named Johnny Bala, who besides being a little fucked up, was absolutely fanatical about his hair. He would spare no expense for the best shampoos, conditioners, combs and brushes, scalp vitamins, and hair dryers with a least twelve temperature settings.

Snapping open his pocket mirror checking out his look, Johnny would pontificate, "If your feathers ain't right, damn it, you ain't right!"

Johnny Bala, what a name. It would be a great name for a secret agent on assignment in some hot spot in the world. When we were growing up, all the guys wished their name was Johnny Bala (especially the guys named Casmir Levandowski, Stosh Stukowski and Thaddeus Lahovwicz). Can you imagine the trauma of walking around with names like that?

Johnny was so cool back then. Sun-glassed and suave, and he had this flair when he lit his cigarette. All the good-looking girls wanted to get a date with Johnny Bala. So suave and handsome was Johnny, that in his senior year of high school he went to four proms with four different girls. On the other hand, there I was just trying to get a date for my prom.

I called Diane from a phone booth in a corner drug store. Waiting for her to pick up, I was trying to build up my confidence.

"Hello." Her voice was like poetry. Sheer beautiful poetry. I was like a bowl of Jell-O and my insides were churning and I could hardly get a word out. She had blonde hair and blue eyes and high cheek bones and I dreamed about her every night, yes, every single night, and I just wanted to get my Dad's car and get her in the back seat in some secluded area and engage in some serious lip locking and whatever might come next.

I stammered. I think I was choking on something. "Diane....would you like to... maybe.......please.... (I tried to clear my throat).

Ah.....go to my...Ah... Senior Prom with me? I'll rent a tux...What kinda flowers do you like? It's in...Ah... a big hotel downtown somewhere in the city. And I would be (cough...cough) honored...if you...would maybe. "

Diane waited all of a micro-second to respond, "I'm going to the prom with Johnny Bala. And who is this anyhow? Do I know you? How did you get my number?"

I was crushed in the phone booth in the corner drug store. I didn't care if a runaway bus came crashing through the corner drug store and smashed the phone booth, with me it, into a million pieces.

I shifted my approach. That's the logical way to do things if something goes askew. Circumvent things, go in a different direction.

"Diane?...do...you...please...have...a......

friend…. who might like to go to a prom…. in a hotel in… the downtown part of the city…. And I'll buy them a corsage?" I'm saying to myself before she can answer.

"Please…For god sakes!… please!…have a friend who wants to go."

I mean I didn't want to be hanging on the corner on prom night and all the guys would ask me,"What's the matter with you? Aren't you going to the prom? Can't you get a date? Are you some kind of a loser?"

"I'm sorry. I have a few girlfriends but they're all depressed because Johnny wouldn't go to their prom, so they're not going to any prom at all. I'm sorry but I have to run. Johnny's coming over to take me out to the new taco restaurant and bowling, and then to the drive-in movie over in New Jersey. I can't wait to get to the drive-in."

I felt so rejected at that moment.

"Bye……Maybe I'll see you at the prom, if you get lucky."

"What's your name anyhow? I don't think I even know you."

Come on bus! Come on! Smash this phone booth to pieces!

Everybody thought that Johnny was going

to go on to great things.

Maybe a hip talking Dee Jay on a hot hits radio station.

Could be a fashion model with a portfolio of eight-by-ten glossies.

Maybe a leading man in the movies.

I thought he was going to be just your basic everyday jerk-off.

Now I was never bitter or hostile towards Johnny just because he shafted me on my senior prom. No! Not at all! I'm not that kind of a person.

I did go to the prom. I had a friend who had a sister and she volunteered to go with me. Her name was Helen. I had a miserable time with Helen that night. I thought that after I spent all of that money to rent a tux and patent leather shoes and the flowers that I should at least have a good time and maybe get some passionate kisses and maybe a little feel job. But oh no! Helen said, "I'm not that kind of a girl."

Johnny and Diane were voted most attractive couple at the prom. So they slow danced alone in the spotlight and Johnny kissed her and I could swear I could see some tongue action going on. And I sat there at the table by myself sucking on ice cubes. Helen went off somewhere, and I said to myself, *If it wasn't for that louse, Johnny Bala, I coulda been something at this prom with Diane. They would've played a love song and I would hold Diane real close and I would've got all worked up. But no! She's out there on the dance floor with that no good Johnny Bala and I'm here by myself sucking on ice cubes.*

Mambo King

Actually, years later, Johnny had some deep psychological problems that had him completely screwed up (we'll get into this a little later) but he thought he could overcome them and walk in the sunshine with an aura of confidence if he could only become the "Mambo King" at the *Learn To Dance And Be Popular Dance Club* where he played flamenco guitar on a part-time basis.

Johnny needed the extra money. He was twice-married and twice-divorced and both wives had these ball-busting lawyers and they took everything that Johnny had. And Johnny had to park his piece of junk car five blocks away because he sensed that the finance company was coming in the middle of the night and they were going to hook his car up to a tow truck.

Now everybody needs an aura of confidence

once in a while in their life when everything is crashing in on them. Who doesn't want to walk in the sunshine and exclaim, "Damn! I feel real good about myself! I'm going to take on the world and do some great things!" Most guys do it some other way though. A great career. Money in the bank. A beautiful wife.

But if being the "Mambo King" did it for Johnny, so be it.

Johnny worked full-time as a travel agent in a high up office tower in Center City and his office had a great view of the museums along the Parkway, which he never visited or did he give a fuck as to what was inside them. Johnny was always a little smart-mouthed and at the travel agency he had a hard time dealing with stressed out people who would come in trying to get away from some of the things that can fuck up your life.

They would come in and start moaning, "We don't know where we want to go. We're stressed out and we need relaxation. Maybe the mountains out west? How about one of the oceans? We've never been to South America."

Tapping his pen in annoyance on his desk at the same time leaning forward and aggressively turning pages of a travel brochure, Johnny's totally pissed off. He's saying to himself. *Just get the hell out of my office and don't get hit by a bus outside.*

Johnny never developed any real selling skills making potential customers feeling welcomed and uplifted at the travel agency using energized statements like:

"Welcome to our agency!"

"We're so glad that you're here!"

"With us, service is number one!"

"We'll match you with the right destination anywhere on the face of the earth so that your aura completely changes!"

Another question from the moaning couple, "How about somewhere in Europe where there's some castles and moats and maybe they...what do they call it?...show you what the Knights of the Round Table did with Lady...what was her name?" Now this yuppie couple wearing their European style clogs came to the travel agency seeking some advice from a travel agent expert wanting a great suggestion so they could go somewhere and come back feeling completely refreshed and take on their high-pressured jobs and their screaming kids.

For some reason, Johnny hated anyone who wore European style clogs. He thinks they're the same haughty high-society people who look down on everyone else and they go to coffee shops and order these Grande caramel sugar-free extra-hot decaf lattes with a little cinnamon on the top, and the coffee-making people have to use these machines that sound like jet plane engines revving up.

About a month later, Johnny was shown the door at the travel agency and he took his sarcastic attitude and tried to sell steel-toed work boots in a rundown strip center inside the city that catered to the low I.Q. crowd. The final straw at the agency happened when Johnny told a customer wearing European style clogs, "Why don't you just throw a dart at the map on the wall and wherever the dart lands, go there! And stop breaking my stones!"

Anyone could enter the Mambo Dance Contest. Even members of the band could enter the Mambo Dance Contest. Johnny was kind of suave with his olive complexion and his black hair slicked back. And he had this put-on western European accent and he thinks his dancing partner would have it in her mind that he was somehow related to a Spanish Count.

Johnny could actually see himself out there on the dance floor. He really could. Sultry, perspiring, beautiful thing in his arms, her black hair pulled back tightly highlighting her sensual face with high cheekbones and intelligent eyes and her beautiful shapely legs coming out from her tight red skirt slit up to where Johnny wants to get his hands, and oh god!—those black leather stiletto heels.

The throbbing, pulsating, mambo dance music's coming from every direction. Johnny called it "Zorro Music." Dance floor lights are swirling. Johnny's out there in his formal tuxedo. His shiny black patent leather shoes gliding over the dance floor. He overdid his best cologne and hair spray, and he's thinking he might get laid later on.

It's the grand finale crescendo moment. The crowd is breathless. Johnny spins her out, they stand there motionless, striking a pose for about two heartbeats, she comes swirling back! Breathlessly! Arms high aloft and she throws her left leg high in the air her stiletto heel motionless! Johnny grabs her waist and her upper leg offering support and he gazes deep into her eyes hoping she catches his drift about getting laid.

The music stops and the place goes fucking nuts.

"YEA! YEA! THE MAMBO KING!" Everybody is shouting and cheering. The place is still going nuts and everyone shouts in unison,
"ENCOR! ENCOR! DO IT AGAIN MAMBO KING!"

The ovation gets louder and louder.

"DO IT AGAIN MAMBO KING!"

After taking some deep bows in the spotlight trying to look like Fred Astaire, Johnny suggests to his dancing partner, her name is Jolene, that maybe they should go outside for a while and relax in the back seat of his 1999 Buick Regal and then come back in and hear the judge's decision.

Jolene tells Johnny if he thinks he's going to get anything in the back seat of a 1999 Buick, he's out of his mind, and outside of the dance floor she wants nothing to do with someone who should be fitted with some elevator shoes and up close the hair piece just isn't working. All Jolene wanted to do is win a trophy or two and get some free dance lessons.

That's all Jolene wanted. Some free dance lessons and a cheap trophy. And if she used Johnny to get them, so what. She knew Johnny wasn't the tallest guy around. She knew his hair was thinning out. She knew this. And yet, she just used him.

Are people in this world totally without morals? Using someone just to pick up a cheap trinket.

Johnny just stood there and his whole miserable life just flashed in front of him and the psychological scars he wore were festering as he watched Jolene walk over and start to talk to Rudy, who plays the bongo drums in the Mambo Dance Band. It was a real scene. Johnny's just standing there by himself in the spotlight, and Jolene's trying to hit on the guy playing the bongo drums.

The miserable bitch, using Johnny like that. You had to feel sorry for him standing there by himself in the spotlight. And the phobias that have tormented him for years and years, being too short and the thinning hair, just hit him like a bolt of lightning right there on the dance floor.

And his feelings came out. Rivers and rivers of them.

"Please! Whoever has anything to do with this, please let me win!"

"Give me the Mambo King Trophy and let me walk in the sunshine."

"Let me have a sense of pride about myself."

Things got worse for Johnny after that night. This just what he needed. He visited his hair doctor two days later and the news wasn't good. The hair doctor was a real prick. No sympathy whatsoever for the pathetic figure in his office. Holding some x-ray photos up to a spotlight, he shook his head, lit a cigarette, and he just tossed the x-ray photos on his desk. And he just blurted it out.

"Sorry Johnny. Sorry. It's M.P.B. Male Pattern Baldness. It's hopeless. And you're not a good candidate for a hair weave job."

It was sad to see Johnny walking home by himself, tears welling up in his eyes. Then he gets home and there's a certified letter in his mailbox.

Dear Valued Customer,

We are sorry to inform you that the Acme Elevator Shoe Company is going out of business. It just seems like there aren't too many short people around anymore. Thank you for your business over the past fifteen years. We have a company under our umbrella that has just put some growth hormone pills on the market. Please find enclosed some free samples.

Sincerely,

C. S. Eshington, President.

Uncle Clyde Bala

Rudy and Jolene hit it off pretty good and things got serious with them. Jolene always had the hots for any guy who played in a band, as long as he wasn't a midget. Rudy loved stiletto heels and fishnet stockings. Johnny started to stalk Jolene and she had him served with a restraining order. Even with the restraining order, he stalked her again as Jolene was leaving a tanning and body waxing salon and he did a couple of days in jail.

Feeling this deep pain after everything that happened to him, Johnny thought it would be best if he just went far away. He needed a change, a new direction, he wanted to elevate himself to a new life. He was thinking about moving to Montana and joining a Back-To-Nature-Commune and they had tents in the forest and they could only nourish themselves with nuts and berries which were abundant in the deep woods.

Somehow though, through a tragic event, salvation from that. Johnny saw an ad for a business opportunity in the classified section of the Sunday paper. The business opportunity required a five-thousand-dollar down payment. Johnny and his twin brother, Charles Remington Bala, (A.K.A. Chucky) put up the down payment from money they inherited from their uncle, Clyde Bala, who suffered a fatal slip and fall accident unloading fruit from a South American freighter docked at the piers on the waterfront. Uncle Clyde took a swan dive to the bottom of the ship where the bananas had just been removed and Clyde hit solid steel and splattered a little bit. As a matter of fact, Clyde splattered a lot.

For their investment, Johnny and Chucky went into the home security alarm business. They got a red step-up van, complete home security systems special high-powered batteries to attach to the security systems in case a customer's power went out, and manuals and tools and ladders to help install the systems.

And the most important thing they received: A police report of at least three-hundred people who have had their homes broken into and cleaned out in the Tri-State area.

They had the sides of their truck stenciled: *Bala Brothers Home Security. We Keep The Thugs Out.*

Johnny checked the list and he noticed someone who had their home broken into and cleaned out close to the New Jersey Pine Barrens. He got an idea and he ran it by Chucky.

"Why not try and sell this guy who got his home busted into around the Pine Barrens a security system, and at the same time we can try and catch the Jersey Devil. If we catch the Jersey Devil they'll make a T. V. special about us and we'll be on all the talk shows."

Chucky thought about it for a second. "Great idea! Let's do it!"

Legend has it that the Jersey Devil is some kind of a vicious monster with sharp teeth and claws who has been scurrying around the New Jersey Pine Barrens for over a hundred years or so. Johnny and Chucky went out and bought some items they thought they would need to catch the Jersey Devil.

They bought a baseball bat just in case they had to sedate the Jersey Devil. Some rope to tie him up and restrain him with. Two flashlights because they were going to do it late at night, and Johnny read somewhere that the Jersey Devil slept most of the day and he was more active at night which, Johnny felt, would make him easier to find. And they bought about thirty pounds of frozen chicken legs which were on sale at the *Shop Thrifty Store* on Frankford Avenue. They were going to toss the chicken legs into the woods to entice the Jersey Devil. For courage, and refreshment and maybe to settle their nerves, they bought two cases of top shelf wine coolers. After all, they never went monster hunting before.

Johnny said, "Let's just go after the Jersey Devil first, and if we get him we'll be rich and we'll never have to sell an alarm system."

Chucky snapped open a wine cooler. He quickly drank half of the bottle, and he reasoned. "That's a good idea. Because I don't know a damn thing about puttin' in alarm systems."

Around midnight, Johnny drove over the Tacony Palmyra Bridge and headed over Route 73 towards the Pine Barrens. The wine cooler bottles in the back of the truck were clattering around. Chucky said they sounded like a musical instrument, but he wasn't sure which one it was. After about ninety minutes, and two wine coolers each, they hit the New Jersey Pine Barrens.

"Let's celebrate, we're here!" Chucky cried out. "Let's crack open two more then let's get famous."

It was dark on the road slicing through the deep woods.

Breaking balls, Johnny turned the headlights off to play with Chucky.

Animals were making strange sounds.

"Damn it, Johnny!   Stop playing around!"

Laughing like an idiot, Johnny turned the headlights back on.

They didn't see any road leading into the Pine Barrens.

Chucky was losing his courage.

A state trooper patrol cruiser went by in the other direction.

Losing bravado, Chucky said, "Let's just sell alarm systems."

On his left, up ahead, Johnny saw a clearing in the woods. It was nothing more than two ruts leading into the deep woods. He turned left and the van started to bounce around like crazy, and neither one of them saw the "NO TRESPASSING" sign nailed to a tree. The van careened around as if it was an amusement park ride and Chucky thought he heard the sound of breaking glass coming from the wine cooler cases.

After about five-hundred feet into the deep woods, the van hit a rock or an animal carcass and a front tire blew out and it sounded like an explosion. The van sagged to one side and Chucky blurted out, "What the hell are we going to do now?"

Johnny was on a mission and he wasn't giving up and he wasn't thinking about changing a flat tire. Instead, he downed half of another wine cooler to help settle his nerves.

"Just calm the hell down! I'll do the rest. You just stay here! "Johnny exclaimed, getting out of the van wearing pointed-toe black dress shoes, a midnight blue silk shirt, and a pair of black dress slacks he wore when he got married for the second time. He wanted to be properly dressed just in case he had to start selling alarm systems if the Jersey Devil thing didn't work out.

Johnny got the flashlight and the baseball bat. He put about two dozen chicken legs in a shopping bag. He told Chucky to wave the flashlight outside the window as a beacon, and he started to walk into the deep woods making some animal sounds trying to mimic the Jersey Devil and draw him out of the woods. There were scary animal sounds in the woods, it was pitch black dark, and Chucky was waving the flashlight and he was scared to death and just then a bat flew by and he almost dropped the flashlight.

Chucky was way out of his element in the deep woods. He had a bad experience while out on bivouac as part of his two week military obligation during a blistering hot summer in South Carolina a few years ago. Chucky woke up about midnight to take a piss; he turned on his flashlight, and crawling on the sides of his tent were about twenty daddy long leg spiders. Actually, the spiders weren't crawling on the sides of the tent, they were eerily bouncing around on their long legs.

In his panic to eject himself from his tent,

Chucky stood up and he ripped the tent pegs from the ground. So there's Chucky hollering and screaming spiders all over him; he's waking up military personnel, and he decides to try to run away from everything which was a bad idea because the tent is wrapped around his head. Chucky ran about fifty feet and he ran head first into a tree and he knocked himself stone cold out. Chucky suffered a slight concussion and they had to Medevac him out of the deep woods. He came out of everything okay. Although, he had this distant look in his eyes. It's like you think someone's home, but no one answers the door.

Johnny was tossing chicken legs into the woods, at the same time making animal sounds trying to duplicate what he thought the Jersey Devil would sound like. He was about fifty feet from the van when the molechuk got him around the back of his leg, and Johnny thought it was the Jersey Devil who got him. Johnny wanted to scream out but the pain was too much and he felt like he couldn't breathe. He dropped everything, and he staggered towards Chucky who figured out that something was wrong and maybe they won't get famous after all.
"THE JERSEY DEVIL GOT ME! THE JERSEY DEVIL GOT ME!"
"GO AFTER HIM BEFORE HE GET'S AWAY!

"GO GET HIM CHUCKY! HE'S IN THE WOODS SOMEWHERE!"

Chucky said to himself, *Fuck that!* Johnny fell like a brick.

And who knows how some things happen and maybe it would have been nice to have an electrician there to explain some things. Maybe the leaking wine coolers sloshing around the back of the van short-circuited the batteries and the alarm systems. Anyhow, some of the alarm systems went off and they gave off this blaring sound and it reverberated through the trees and you couldn't even hear the animal sounds anymore.

Chucky was trying to help Johnny get up when the state police cruiser pulled up behind the van. Johnny fell back into the dirt gasping and just like that he said it felt like his heart was pounding. The police officer, flashlight in hand wearing his starched uniform, got out of his cruiser and he was pissed off because someone was screwing around in the woods he had to patrol and he might have to waste his time doing some paperwork because of a couple of idiots.

The police officer was not impressed with what he saw. The officer was used to chasing drug runners or catching escaped convicts and there was Johnny on the ground thrashing about, kicking

201

chicken legs around at the same time. The wine coolers he drank hit Chucky and he was staggering around almost walking off into the deep woods.

For his own good, the police officer handcuffed Chucky and put him in the back seat of the police cruiser. Helping Johnny get up, noticing his pointed-toe dress shoes and his blue silk shirt and tight fitting slacks, the police officer asked him, "What's going on here Mr. Dance Fever? At least give me a reason for taking you in so I don't think you're just plain stupid."

Johnny mumbled to the police officer, "I know how many alarm systems are in the van. I counted them." Just what the police officer wanted to hear, being accused of being a possible thief... this coming from a screwball from the city. Johnny got handcuffed to Chucky in the back seat just in case they would try to jump out of the cruiser.

On the way to the hospital, Johnny yanked on the handcuffs pulling Chucky closer. He struggled to get the words out...slurring them. "Tell Jolene all is forgiven in getting me locked up...Sent to jail...And it's okay with me if she wants to hit on me...If...she...wants...to...I'm...here...for...her."

Startled, Chucky asked, "Jolene...who? What? Don't get me involved with your screwed up friends."

Late the next afternoon, the E.R. doctor told Johnny he was a lucky guy. He told Johnny that the alcohol in the wine coolers probably slowed down the deadly venom from the molechuk and it stopped it from surging throughout his body. "Molechuk venom can be pretty bad," the doctor explained, then releasing Johnny, giving him a prescription and advising him at the same time to try and have a good life. On the spur of the moment, realizing he was dealing with a screwball, the E.R. doctor added a direct and to-the-point tone to his voice. "It would be a good idea if you went under some psychological counseling right now. Right now! It seems like you've done some stupid things and you don't want to screw yourself up anymore."

According to the Animal Institute of America (A.I.A.) located in Washington D. C., Johnny was lucky that he got bit by the more docile and less-venomous molechuk indigenous to the northern states rather than getting bit by the molechuk's more vicious and more venomous counterpart found in the southern states.

Somehow, Chucky got a local service station to tow the van out of the woods and fix the front tire. He tossed the summons for trespassing in a trash dumpster and he went to pick Johnny up at the hospital.

Johnny was sitting in bright sunlight on a bench outside the E.R. entrance and he was deep in thought as if something profound had just happened to him and he may have seen the light about a couple of things. Johnny got in the van and he just sat there in silence watching some squirrels scampering around the parking lot.

Chucky pleaded, "Let's just sell some alarms! Okay!"

Still in silence, in deep thought, analyzing everything that happened, Johnny then lit a cigarette. He took a deep drag then this, "Wanna hear what that doctor told me?...Wanna hear what he said?...Know what he said?"

Chucky just looked at the squirrels and then at Johnny. "No. What?"

"He said I'm really screwed up in the head. He said I need psychological counseling right now...right now before I really fuck myself up. I gotta hook up with a lawyer. I've been the victim of medical malpractice and evaluation of the worse kind."

8,000 B. T. U. Air-conditioner

"Just about five minutes and you're next," Vince advised me. "By the way, there's something in there about them finding the Captain of the Titanic on an iceberg in the ocean and he's still alive floating around after all these years."

There it was. PAGE ONE. Letters big and bold with pictures.

I glanced at page one and something just caught my eye. It was right above the picture of a waxy looking victim of a vampire bite at rest in his coffin. The headlines jumped out and announced, "Flaming Meteors Falling to Earth from Outer Space. Do not Attempt to Catch Them, Scientists Warn!" And right below that, "5,000 Year Old Egyptian Mummy with Soiled Mummy Wrap Loose in the City."

I don't know why. I saw the picture of the mummy and what's this about flaming meteors falling from outer space, and somehow I thought back to the great 8,000 B.T.U. air-conditioner catching event that took place years ago when I was much younger and more impressionable.

What an event it was; I'll never, never forget it.

In the mid-1980's, Bill *Tiger* Stukowski and his twin brother, Andy, each in their mid-30's, would often stop around Smica's Corner to converse with the younger guys who hung out there. *Tiger* and Andy were the uncles of someone who hung on the corner, but I can't recall who could claim that family lineage. It may have been Johnny Rat or the *Big Cad*, but I'm not sure.

Wait. It could have been, Taboo, who was pretty good at dancing the Killer Stomp, but I'm not sure of that either.

Actually, all the guys first started to hang out at Smica's Corner, but we had to relocate across the street to Bulboff's Corner, which was actually a produce and vegetable corner store located at the corner of Stiles and Margaret Streets in the Frankford section of the city. The reason for the relocation was this: Mr. and Mrs. Smica ran a very successful corner grocery store, and they had a pretty prim-and-proper daughter named Madeline. Mr. and Mrs. Smica put their daughter on a pedestal thinking she was a darling princess and because they charged the highest prices in the neighborhood, they sent her to private school and they had high hopes for her future. Madeline had the latest fashion styles purchased at the best dress and shoe salons on Frankford Avenue.

The last thing the Smicas wanted was for

any of the guys who hung on their corner to start sniffing around their daughter. So every time we would hang on his corner, Mr. Smica would come out and hose his pavement down. Or he would complain to the neighborhood committeeman calling the guys hanging on his corner delinquents and the police should come and chase them away. So after realizing we overstayed our welcome outside his corner grocery store, we just moved across the street.

Actually, I had my eye on Madeline. And I had this thought that she might like to go with me to my High School Spring Carnival. I thought that me and Madeline could engage in some pleasant conversation at the spring carnival and it would be a night away from the mindless chit-chat on the corner. The thing was this, how do I get to ask Madeline directly?

I came up with a plan. So I went about two steps into the grocery store; I saw Mr. Smica there slicing roast beef for a customer and I ran out and knocked on their side door hoping Madeline would answer. The door opened about six inches, and I couldn't believe it, Mr. Smica was there glaring at me. I couldn't believe that he figured out my plan.

Quickly, I built up some courage. "I would

like......to.....Could...I...ask...your.....daughter.....
Madeline ...If she would like to go with me to my
High School Spring Carnival?"

Ronnie the *Big Cad*, was hanging on
Bulboff's Corner with Johnny Rat, and he yells at
me. "Are you nuts trying to ask her out? She's too
uppity for you."

Mr. Smica was somewhat polite. He yells
behind the door. "Madeline, do you want to go to a
spring carnival with this guy?"

I'm trying to get some words out, "Tell her it's
me," after he said the word "Guy."

Mr. Smica fired this like a bullet, "SHE SAID
NO!" and he slammed the door in my face. It's funny,
but since I got the door slammed in my face, I never
had the urge to date anyone named Madeline.

Madeline's prim-and-proper image held up
pretty good until her second year at college. She got
knocked up pretty good and it was with a guy who
didn't even attend a private school.

So it's about a month later and I pretty much
recovered from the Johnny Bala and Diane prom
incident and I told everybody in the neighborhood,
"Don't patronize Smica's store because their roast
beef is rancid." Actually, that made me feel pretty
good.

It's a sweltering Saturday in August, at least ninety-eight degrees, and all the guys are hanging on the corner sweating and thinking about where we could go today to meet some girls. Like that was really going to happen, ten guys would go somewhere and meet ten girls on a sweltering day.

Johnny Rat said, "Let's go to New York."

Sonka the *Tailor* replied, "Are you nuts?"

Ronnie the *Big Cad* was there with his bulldog, Brutus. Brutus was snarling at something only he could see and the *Big Cad* had him leashed to a fire hydrant. Clacky and Barookie came around and said we should all go swimming at the Boulevard Pools because there's plenty of girls there.

Lenny Blazer did the math: "Yeah! And there's a thousand guys there too."

Clacky and Barookie went to the Boulevard Pools and they got sun poisoning and blisters and they didn't meet any girls.

Just then, following a Route J bus, first the stench then a tractor trailer filled with cows, mooing forlornly, on their way to the slaughter house on Aramingo Avenue. No sooner had the forlornly mooing cows cleared the intersection and who crosses the street but the Stukowski twins, *Tiger* and

Andy.

Tiger and Andy were bar hopping, chain smoking, laughing at each other's simple jokes, and then, here they are. Tiger tells the Big Cad if Brutus doesn't stop snarling he was going to kick his fucking head in.

Tiger emphasized, "I hate fucking bulldogs!" Actually, Tiger had some patriotic goals in his life back then. He wanted to invade Cuba during the Cuban Embargo Crisis. Besides his brother, Andy, Tiger said he had an army of twenty bar friends who would go with him. Tiger's plans for the invasion were brief and simple. Go to Atlantic City. Rent some fishing boats and head south. Tiger said he would have gone on with the invasion but he didn't want to interfere with the nation's naval blockade of the Cuban island.

So Tiger's standing on Bulboff's Corner sunburned, sweating profusely, chain smoking and cursing the blasted heat. Then squinting through the steamy haze, Tiger spotted a traveling appliance salesman pulling a red wooden wagon up Stiles Street. On the wagon was a decrepit looking air-conditioner with a paper sign taped to it. "IT COOLS GOOD! ONLY SLIGHTLY USED! BEAT THE HEAT! ONLY 50 BUCKS!"

Tiger whistled the traveling appliance

salesman over. "I'll give you twenty-five bucks cash right now!" *Tiger* exclaimed wiping sweat from his forehead with the back of his hand before pulling out a wad of dollar bills from his pocket. *Tiger* starts counting them out.

"Okay!" the salesman replied, "but the warranty is cancelled and you can't use the wagon for delivery purposes."

But *Tiger*," Andy interrupted, "you don't know anything about putting an air-conditioner in."

Tiger bristled, "Don't worry. I'll guide you in putting the air-conditioner in. I can't take this heat anymore and it's messing up my thought process."

The next time anyone saw *Tiger*, which was about a month later, he was bandaged mummy-style from his chest to his knees. *Tiger's* outstretched arms and his legs were rigid and fighting the pain through clenched teeth he moaned. "I almost caught that sucker. I can't believe that I dropped it. It went right through my arms and it nearly broke my knees and crushed my feet. I wish I had another shot at it. Damn, those air-conditioner vents can tear you up when they pick up some speed."

Noticing *Tiger's* weakened condition, The *Big Cad* asked him, "Are you fucking nuts?"

Anyhow, according to eyewitnesses who witnessed the great air-conditioner catching event (only twenty people saw the event, but over the years hundreds now say they saw it), it went something like this:

After staggering down Margaret Street under the weight of the 8,000 B.T.U. air- conditioner, *Tiger* and Andy lifted the unit clamoring up the steps to *Tiger's* second-floor apartment on Tacony Street. Exhausted, they shared a cold six-pack to cool off. Then Andy maneuvered the air-conditioner in *Tiger's* living room window while *Tiger* guided him from the burning pavement below.

Andy pushed and pulled and twisted and turned the air-conditioner cursing *Tiger* all the while. Shielding his eyes from the hot sun, *Tiger* screamed up at Andy. "Do this! Try that! Twist it! Turn it! Push it out!"

Then, god no...please...perish the thought, the unthinkable happened. Andy lost control of the air-conditioner and it plummeted out of the second story window. Andy yelled out the window, "IT SLIPPED! IT JUST SLIPPED! WATCH OUT BELOW!"

Witnesses gasped and covered their eyes. Then total insanity took over on Tacony Street. Total damn insanity.

His arms outstretched, *Tiger* tried to catch the air-conditioner that was zeroing in on him like a meteor from a black hole in outer space. The unit bounced off his chest and ricocheted through his arms and between his legs.

In *Tiger*'s defense, however, in lieu of his service contract, he did have twenty-five bucks invested in the appliance.

Tiger was in intensive care for a week. Psychological counseling was provided. They asked, "You did what? YOU DID WHAT?"

Body cast and all, *Tiger* couldn't wait to get home from the hospital. The first thing that he did when he got home was to gather all of his friends, the same ones who were going to invade Cuba with him. *Tiger* told them to go out and find the traveling air-conditioner salesman with the red wooden wagon and beat the living hell out of him.

Tiger just wanted to get even with the guy who sold him an air-conditioned that didn't fit in his living room window.

"You're next, Ron," Vince the Barber exclaimed noticing the nostalgic look on my face.

Somehow, I felt compelled to tell Vince everything about *Tiger*'s attempt to catch a falling air-conditioner from a second-story window in the mid-1980's.

I told Vince everything. Everything. He looked at me in total disbelief. Like I was trying to trick him or fool him with some simple story.

"That could never happen, Ron. Never! Nobody in the world could be that fucking stupid."

I didn't tell Vince about *Tiger*'s plans to invade Cuba.

Ron Neumer is a former award-winning news reporter and columnist who covered the Northeast section of Philadelphia, PA. Ron resides in Devon PA with his wife, Ginny, and he likes to look out over the trees from his home and be creative.

Email: rneumer54@comcast.net

Made in the USA
Middletown, DE
27 April 2015